Keep Breathing Out

Born an Irish Jew in Dublin, Maurice White graduated in medicine then psychiatry at Trinity College Dublin. Later, he trained and worked as a Kleinien Psychoanalyst at the Institute of Psychoanalysis in London, where he became a Fellow.

While a Consultant at Wormwood Scrubs he treated Sex offenders and Murderers, and also worked in Mental hospitals in Ireland, England and Canada.

A journalist and broadcaster, his hobbies have included backyard pigs and horse racing.

Keep Breathing Out

A Novel by
Maurice White

Kennedy & Boyd

Kennedy & Boyd
an imprint of
Zeticula Ltd
The Roan
Kilkerran
KA19 8LS
Scotland.

http://www.kennedyandboyd.co.uk
admin@kennedyandboyd.co.uk

First published in 2013
Copyright © Maurice White 2013

Cover design from a photograph Copyright © Alan Cotter
2013

ISBN-13 978-1-84921-119-2

For my beloved daughters

Catherine, Jacky, Emma and Molly

Acknowledgements

Thanks and love to all my family and friends.

In particular to Michele Childers and Anne Harries. I owe everything to Gill and to Brenda for their support and inspiration.

And along the years to Judy Cook, Peter Langworth, Ron Wallace, Harold Glass, Al Brown, Nick Daubeny, Richard Sutherland and Lou Lentin.

Also I am indebted for insights into many of life's mysteries to Isobel Menzies, Bernard Gilsenan, Betty Kelleghan, Helen Bellany, Donika Xhixha, Margot Waddell, Eva Sen and Lois Monro.

I also wish to thank all my many patients who opened their lives to me. In particular Dr Jim Hardiman for his many insights into the influences of institutional care on young children.

Maurice White
April 2013

Other people have a nationality
The Irish and the Jews have a psychosis
Brendan Behan (Richard Corkleg Act 1)

The World accepts dangerous experiments in the realm of art because it does not take art seriously: but it condemns them to life.

Jean Cocteau. Le Livre Blanc

When Hitler dropped his second bomb on Ireland, it fell on David Benn's semi-detached house in Terenure. The other one just missed a synagogue on South Circular Road, lending weight to the suspicion that there was more than chance involved in the assault.

Twenty years later, in the early days of spring, David stood at the bar of Dargle's Grand Hotel, some two hundred miles from home. Hardly a round the world tour when all the main roads of the Free State joined together wouldn't stretch the width of France; nevertheless he felt jet-lagged. Four different news programmes on the car radio, all repetitions of the same *mishegass* from Belfast and Tel Aviv. Making connections was one thing (*good for development according to Freud*), spreading a plague of impending disaster was another; even for a Jew. *A Hard Day's Night* had been his favourite tune at the start of the journey.

"I'm looking for the Asylum."

"Saint Elba's is it?" The barman topped up David's pint of Guinness, beckoning towards the window with a slight shrug of his shoulder as he embellished the frothy crown.

"You can't go wrong, Sir. Just follow the main road out of Dargle then look up the hill ahead of you and there it is for all who wish to see. Count Dracula's Castle itself. Am I right, gentlemen?"

The few desultory stragglers from the lunchtime trade at the Grand Hotel lounge bar stared deeply into their almost-empty glasses. Commercial travellers seemed disinclined to return to their clients, a few yards along the High Street.

The optimism that had been rekindled by the start of a new year was long since dead. Foreign imports of ready-mades had done nothing to improve the situation. Even a Greek would be happy here. They have the testicles for tragedy.

"Dublin you're from, Sir?"

"Indeed, I am."

David Benn tilted the glass to his lips. Only two leaves of the shamrock emblazoned in the head of his pint were visible. As he drank they were being sucked into the dark recesses of the creamy liquid. *In spite of the break I'm still suffering. Combat fatigue without a doubt. A finger tip search and not a sign of a pulse beat under the new Kingston's shirt cuff. Lamb dressed as mutton. For a member of the wandering tribe I'm not much of a traveller.*

Two quaffs down he paused again. *A mistake to drop into the hotel bar. This Guinness is not good for me. Maybe it only works on real Irishmen. Perhaps what I need is a few mints to suck before I show my face up there.*

David looked up to see the bartender staring at him.

He thinks I'm the odd-fellow heading for nutty farm. Think away, my friend, but then take a gander at your own place, will you? The fifties décor of faded golden plush looks all of its age. Yet you call yourselves The Grand. You wouldn't have to be a psychiatrist to see the neglect. No self pride.

As he had set out on his journey his father warned him that things would not be too hot outside the capital, adding as an after-thought, that they're not so great inside it either. "Neutrality has left their spirit neutered, even though it's a good thirty years since Dev did his double act with the Swiss."

On the wall, behind the barman, an array of glasses and whiskey bottles multiplied in the dust of the mirror that ran the full length of the counter.

There's your wealth. Write it out in a verse.

Tullamore — Give Everyman His Dew — beside the Middleton, that terrible beauty, twenty year old and yet to be opened. Further down the shelf half full bottles of Paddy, Powers and Jamesons tell a different story. Behind them a lone bottle of Scotch, Johnny Walker Black — a blend —barely visible, awaits a lover from across the water.

Follow the main road he said.

David drove quickly through the town. His mother had taken him to the new school on the number fourteen bus ... lower deck.

What age was I then? All of nine — maybe ten. At the gates — a Protestant establishment for decent boys — the school sergeant (British war medals on his chest) seemed to notice the missing foreskin.

"Are yous Jews?" He had demanded to know, in a tone that spelled trouble.

It had not augured well for my future at that school. Perhaps the sergeant had not known that circumcision was meant as a substitute for human sacrifice and could not be made twice. If only I had possessed the power of my African counterpart, I would have waved a spear at the enemy and shouted 'Amadoda'!

Why had my mother taken me into enemy territory when I was not yet ready for combat?

Slowing down to second gear, he approached the entrance to the asylum.

David had no doubt that his parents equated getting him into that school with a step up the social ladder. In the mirror of his Ford Prefect he glimpsed the city spread out below. A picture the Irish Tourist Board could put in their travel brochure. Clusters of houses fanned out from the river that ran through the centre. They rose in terraces until they blended into neatly tilled farm land that stretched out in the distance to fasten itself to the sky line.

There are tribes I've heard of, since, who practice secret sacrifices for similar reasons, but how would my mother have reacted if my ashes had been delivered to her door? True, she might have been deeply honoured, but as the sacrificial lamb I'd not have been around to join her in the celebrations.

At the open gates of the hospital he followed the signs directing him to the administration office. He braced himself, entered the barn-like room and waited by the doorway. The afternoon sunlight was reflected from oak panelling that lined the walls, enveloping the room in a murky yellow light. Workers' heads bent low over giant desks. He peered deeper into the gloom, then took a step back.

Well, I suppose a locum is not exactly top of the social agenda.

3

He moved boldly forward again.

Maybe it is the light after all. Wait a bit though, there is somebody looking. I can see the whites of her eyes. She's something alright. So relaxed as she moves this way, her head held up to the world like she knows God's on her side. Black hair made blacker by that high neck of her white Aran sweater. All she lacks is an identity crisis. No need to fret, I've enough for both of us.

Deirdre Gillespie beckoned him towards a chair opposite her and introduced herself. The young man seated at the next desk looked up in her direction. She smiled at him, then turned back to hand David a neat batch of forms across her desk. "A hard journey down? Don't worry, this won't take us too long." He signed the papers, glancing up at her for guidance as he turned over the pages.

Another bloody temporary post. In six months time it'll be make way for the local hero who will get the real job and the woman. She'll settle for six of his brats .. or maybe seven to please his mother. Poor unmatched little thing, you'd have to feel sorry for it. David moved his chair closer to the desk. *What is it about this woman? It can't be just her eyes. Not that she'd be interested in me. No, but she'll have those same eyes on the look out for the main chance, no doubt.*

He glared over at her, frowning. "Here are your forms, Deirdre."

Now, there's real daring. Heaven be praised, I've surprised her. She is looking back at me. Her skin is silk. Can I read her thoughts? We psychiatrists have to be good at that. Dublin foreign enough for you no doubt? What would you know about a Jew doctor from a Protestant university?

The young woman leaned across to pick up a folder that lay on the desk in front of him. Her finger nails were painted a dark green.

Holy Mother of God. Those breasts are too good to waste on some greedy brat. Each breath launches them out towards me. Riders to the Sea. David pushed his chair back from the desk, the feet scraping against the wooden floor boards. *Some people can come just by looking at the likes of her. Wouldn't do my psychiatric career much good though if it were to happen to me right now.*

One thing you can't change is being a Jew. Adolph Hitler saw that one off, once and for all. Anyway, Deirdre, that is your name isn't it, I don't suppose you realise it, but I'm not your usual Trinity chap; then possibly all strangers look alike to you? He leaned back as she collected up the papers, glancing around at the other occupants of the office as he waited. *Take a peek at the rest of them, still with their heads down. Over what I wonder?*

Busy trying to fold madness into neat categories that could be locked away with the same key. Sculptured statues in a bronze light that no doubt reflects their thought patterns. They don't see the fingerprint of far-off Russia on me, or smell the odour of Eastern cities through the Guinness. Half the world's Jewry lived in the Russian Pale, impoverished sprawling land. A bit like the Irish except that your Pale was a rich one, full of goodies, so the English grabbed it for themselves and left you outside. Funny how both of us had to make do with the barren land. Something for us to share, my dear.

David looked around the room again while Deirdre searched in the desk drawer. *This lot probably don't even know where the U.S.S.R is on the map, if their geography lessons were at all like mine. Ask me about the twenty six counties and I'll tell you anything.*

"Are you all right, Doctor Benn?" The eyes stared at him again.

"As near to heaven as I'm ever likely to be, thanks to you rescuing me from the murky wastes beyond." David gave his most winning smile as he prepared to leave the office and seek his quarters.

"Here's the key to your house, and you'll need this other bunch for the locked wards. I hope you will be happy in this place." Deirdre returned his smile.

He inhaled her perfume; fuel for his daydreams.

Olfactory systems all in order. Can't afford to neglect God's chosen radar. Maybe he'd sniffed out the secret that Druids and Yids shared between them. All the ancestors hanging in space with time mellowing their differences. Chalk and cheese melting together like the ingredients of a good malt whiskey.

He was Cuchulin making a salmon leap through barriers to learn the ways of love from Scathan and her daughter Utatach.

News of the bomb that had been dropped on David Benn's house was broadcast in the early morning bulletin from Radio Eireann; competing for air time on the world stage with reports on Adolph Hitler, Lord Haw Haw and Winston Churchill. The results of the Shamrock Rovers v Shelbourne match followed immediately after the reports on these non-sporting events. That very moment when the impact occurred, David Benn was dreaming that he was Paddy Coad, Captain of the Rovers — an ace juggler of the ball, if ever there was one. He'd dribbled sweetly past Eddie Gannon, drawn back his right foot and booted the leather full force towards the Ringsenders goal. The explosion of the German bomb happened to coincide with a rapturous outburst of applause from the football spectators at the match. As his house shuddered he'd opened one eye to see the plaster peel away from the walls of his bedroom, his other eye still celebrating a ticker-tape carnival at the Milltown ground. Then they were gone. Hitler must have been warned about his father's deadly accuracy with the rifle!

The Fuhrer's Luftwaffe came in the dead of night: surprise his weapon, just as it had been when he'd marched on his neighbours on the mainland of Europe.

Some of those countries hardly had time to fire a shot. Like Bernard Benn they could only conjure retrospectively with the prospect of how they might have defended themselves if they had been on guard when the attack came. The Irish army, itself, probably lacked a sophisticated radar or early warning system with which they could alert Mr Benn. Besides, they needed all the available intelligence network to help them decide if being neutral meant that every over-flying aeroplane should be regarded as a friend — or an enemy. David's Aunty Hetty, who lived next door, suspected that the house in nearby Templeoge with its swastika shaped roof had helped guide these bombers towards Terenure.

The bomb crater was a centre of interest for a time. Small crowds gathered to look down the hole. Volunteers from the Local Defence Force, caught by surprise, searched in their emergency manual for information on how to deal with the puncture to their neutrality shield. Neighbourhood gangs of children made forts around it to aid them in their own local skirmishes. Gabriele Fallon, head of the Fortfield mob, who'd never so much as given a glance in David's direction before, asked him if he'd got any bits of the bomb he could swap, proffering a worn looking copy of *The Champion* in exchange.

"Why would Hitler waste good bombs on a few Jew-men?"

His father had overheard the remark and told his mother. She grimaced but said nothing. She was busy with her packing for the evacuation around the corner to her parents' house on Terenure Road East — after tidying up her own kitchen as best she could. Freshly made gefilte fish, the diverse mixture of flavours from a varied selection of fishes, the secret of its richness, lay scattered over the floor, knocked from its shelf in the pantry by the force of the bomb blast.

There was little respite for David. One day later he was sent back to his Jewish school in South Circular Road. He'd already overplayed the sympathy card. A delicate ten year old, he had arrived late on the education scene, having missed some three years through battling with another deadly foe, the tubercular baccilus. Even at that tender age he'd sensed the erotic quality of his own deformities. A cavity under his right arm where necrosis had melted his bone; a third orifice, opening doors denied to the overtly wholesome. So, he was somewhat disappointed that few of the Zion School pupils showed much interest in his newly acquired war experiences. He'd affected a discrete limp for a day or two after the event, on the grounds that more people were likely to notice a damaged leg than a deformed arm. Perhaps one, Thelma Fisher, under her Shirley Temple curls, had looked at him with the kind of awe reserved for celebrities. And of course, nosey Marcus wanted to know all the lurid details.

As new dramas hit the headlines David resigned himself to the spotlight moving away from him. Probably his invalid status had already isolated him and earmarked him as an outsider. Sheep did the same thing when one of their flock took ill.

At his Grandparents' house there seemed to be more interest in the outcome of the cards games than what was going on in the world conflict. Playing Solo, his Grandfather warred openly with his best friend, Mister Hermann, over the abundance he'd bid with the hand he'd been dealt. The outcome of the Dunkirk landing required a less urgent solution. In fact, there was little feeling of neutrality in the house. Grandmother stoked the furnace with family gossip.

"Vie is mina Dora's so ferstsuck vith that Stalin fellow. Hadn't he signed up vith Hitler? Goot God. Even Dev didn't put it in writing. Och mere a mench."

She drank the tea from a saucer sucking on spoonfuls of granulated sugar between mouthfuls. "Maybe it's that moustache of his that's the big attraction."

David arranged his few possessions in the two-up/three-down dwelling allotted to him in the extensive grounds of the hospital. From his bedroom window he could see the high four-storey stone blocks that were joined by long limb-like tunnels to the central administration building — temples to the contrariety of the inmates residing in them. All around, vast swards of grassland and flower beds battled to counter the austere greyness cast by these monuments of granite. What mellowing powers the colourful vegetation could muster were enhanced by the names of Saints, all female, bestowed on these larger buildings. A church, with its priest's house attached at right angles, stood on high ground apart from the rest. Further back from the city roads was the hospital farm. Neatly fenced fields provided forage for a herd of cattle grazing blissfully in the shadow of a red brick abattoir. In the outermost corner of the grounds the resident sow, a Large White, wallowed in solitary Buddha-like seclusion. Lacking the burden of consciousness, however, the pig did not have to grapple with the problem of the reincarnation of its soul. It travelled to visit a neighbouring boar when the occasion required, thus, unlike most of the other occupants, she kept a foot on both sides of the high stone wall surrounding Saint Elba's. As David finished hanging up his only jacket in the gigantic wardrobe he heard someone moving downstairs.

"Don't worry, Doctor! It's only me, Nellie Collins, your helper."

She stood waiting, as her new charge hurried down to inspect his visitor. The middle-aged woman, dressed in faded fawn tweed skirt and woollen matching sweater with a headscarf that partially concealed her face, looked away from the doctor as she spoke.

"It's not the best of houses, sir, but it's not the worst of them either. If you need anything, all you have to do is to ring Saint

Ursula's ward and ask for me, otherwise I'll come over from time to time to clean up a bit, like I do for the others. I'll give two little knocks on your front door so you'll know it's me.' She pointed proudly at a faded brown leather bag that lay by the kitchen door. "I've got my own dusters and things and you've no need to worry yourself on that account."

Twenty years in the asylum had hardly altered Nellie. Certification had been instigated by the brothers she so diligently cared for, and 'arranged' shortly after they discovered she was pregnant. The sexual act had seemed little more to her than an extension of the compliance she had been taught by her siblings. One glimpse of the baby as it left her body was all she had managed. Its father departed unidentified to America, the boat fare paid by his mother. Two decades later, with the security of full board and lodgings, she had little incentive to leave hospital. Her son, unable to dodge the draft, was despatched to the front line in Vietnam with the regulation case of Coca Cola, allegedly reported by an unidentified medical foundation as a source of comfort for babies torn prematurely from their mother's breast.

David completed unpacking the dozen bottles of wine from Finlaters of Rathmines, arranging them side by side, with the more expensive claret concealing the Spanish Burgundy. Next, he placed one bottle of Jameson on the sideboard and the second one in the cupboard before turning back to rearrange the wine so that it was the claret which was hidden from view. Drawing the well-worn easy chair close to the fire, he took a few sods of peat from the neat stack by the fireplace and laid them on the coal and wood fire that Nellie had lit for him, leaning back to admire the conflation.

At least inert materials do not share the same antagonisms that humans exhibited towards each other. Maybe that's what Hitler had in mind when he stoked his furnaces. Just a way of helping people get on together. Thankfully, not so drastic a solution is called for in this place. All that seems to be expected of me, here in Dargle, is to help isolate these 'awkward' individuals who speak in a manner that does not correspond with those outside the walls.

He poked the fire drawing the embers to the centre of the grate, and reached out to pick up another piece of turf. As he did so a rat the size of a ferret dashed across the room, vanishing through a gap at the base of the door where the wood had rotted.

The barman could well have been right about the house of Dracula.

The first morning's round was led by Doctor Francis Reilly. Five foot four, his pointed head and beady features gave him a gnome-like appearance. Neatly suited, he sported a red spotted handkerchief which hung extravagantly from his breast pocket. He met with a select few of the senior staff on some waste ground behind the flower beds. Jerking his head impatiently and making pointed glances at his wrist-watch, he conducted the ritual task of the day — the recording, for his management committee, of evidence that he had seen most of the two thousand inhabitants of the asylum at least twice in that week. The swarthy frame of Wilfred Behan, Chief Nurse — his neck measurements closely challenged his boss's chest girth — moved forward to review the motley army of inmates who were lined up ready to begin their march past. He moved as always, unhurried, beside the Superintendent, taking one step to the smaller man's three or four, responding in a quiet voice to the shrill questions thrown at him. His ubiquitous dark blue suit sat easily on square shoulders. Every now and then one of the two assistant nurses who accompanied the staff contingent went over to address an inmate in the line, then recorded their findings in a notebook.

The long queue of men, whose grey jackets and trousers might once have matched each other, trooped past their keepers with varying degrees of interest. Some stared back at the staff quizzically, as if they too were waiting to receive an important message, while others ignored their presence.

"Everything here, Doctor Benn, from Jesus Himself to that

giant of a man, the High Court judge over there." Behan spoke softly, turning to address his Superintendent.

"Better watch out, His Honour looks as though he is about to put the black cap on your head the way he's eyeing you up."

He smiled at Doctor Reilly. "Indeed, and it's hard to tell sometimes which of us is living in the make-believe world."

The little man snorted but stepped back a pace before twisting around sharply in David's direction.

"Take a good look at that fellow beyond. He imagines that he is Christy Ring the great hurler." They watched as the Hurler swung an unseen stick through the air. His arms twirled this way and that with lightning dexterity. Every few seconds he struck an equally invisible puck, as he darted in and out of the line of unconcerned marchers.

"Good luck for the match." Doctor Reilly shouted before addressing his staff in a solemn tone. "Watch the young lad, he may look the real McCoy but his ticker is a wee bit suspect — he's collapsed on us more than once, and that's no fantasy." David opened his mouth to reply but his senior had turned towards a tall black-cloaked figure at the rear of the procession.

Reilly addressed the figure. "Have you met our new locum, Father? He's come all the way from Dublin, so we're relying on him to show us some of the latest tricks of the trade.

Before the priest could speak, David found himself burbling, "Well, it's true I've heard of one such skill, Doctor Reilly, though I can't claim that Dubliners discovered it. Listening, it's called, but I'm sure you've heard tell of it, Father."

The priest beamed down at him and crushed his hand in a gigantic fist. "There's not many that can bear to practise the forgotten art — though Wilfred here is one of the few I've met that has the shoulders for it." Behan raised a hand in protest. "He is modest with it but I'd say this now, Doctor, that you'll be as much in demand as Himself there if word gets out — and not just from the patients either," the Priest continued. "Bye the way, it's Fintan Dunbar. Even priests have a private tag, ye know. Well, I'll be off now and let you get on. God bless you all." He gave them his blessing with a hurried sign of the cross, then turned and walked towards the church.

"Have you ticked off all the names of that lot in the register, nurse?" Without waiting for a reply, the superintendent strode off towards the wards.

On entering Saint Ethna's they were greeted by the charge nurse, Sarah Nolan.

"You're very welcome, doctor. We have plenty of work for you here." David met the nurse's appreciative smile, but his eyes were drawn beyond her, to a carpet of mattresses on which recumbent bodies covered with gray blankets were strewn out on the floor.

"How are you, Vini?" Doctor Reilly had sprung into action. He withdrew a packet of cigarettes from his pocket and threw a Wills Woodbine in the direction of one of the mattresses. David stared in disbelief. An outstretched hand shot from under a blanket to snatch the cigarette out of the air then vanish from sight.

The next moment it was Sarah, awaiting her cue, who stepped forward, uncurling a long rubber tube and inserting it swiftly down the gullet of a man who was seated in a chair his neck fully extended backwards. Mahatma Ghandi — it was a fellow patient, diagnosed manic depressive, who had given him his nickname — gaping toothless jaw hanging open, signalled his impatience by pointing to the funnel in Sarah's hand.

"It's time he gave this up," murmured Sarah frowning at her patient. "Maybe you'll have the answer, Doctor Benn. It would save us all a great deal of time if you were able to wean him off it." She poured the Complan and milk mixture down the tube and the liquid feed trumpeted its entry into his duodenal passage. 'Gurgles of outflow.'

"Looks like the Indian rope trick in reverse." David ventured, but Doctor Reilly, at the head of his entourage, was already zapping his way towards the padded cells, past the luncheon trolleys lined up in the corridor, the air sodden with the smell of boiled cabbage and waterlogged potatoes.

Wilfred Behan had moved to the front of the group, his staff forming themselves into a protective semicircle behind him as he opened the door of one of the pads an inch or two wide. David caught a glimpse of a white haired figure cloaked in a coarse grey cotton gown — it could have been a prayer shawl on one of those Holy men who doven the synagogue — that reached below his knees but exposed two scrawny ankles and bare feet. His features were unmistakenly semitic.

"Fucking meshuggener stinking goyem bastard pisher nudick nebbech vos macstu tochas Licker." From the freedom of his cell, Cravich hurled his words through the crack, releasing himself of the stored up bitterness he had saved for his few moments in the spotlight.

Quickly the door was slammed closed, distancing the alien shrieks to a mere whisper. An assistant nurse entered the sighting of Cravich in his notebook.

The Chief dropped back to walk beside the new locum as the carousel of therapists wended their way through the rest of the saintly blocks. "I dare say you have seen the likes of all this before, Doctor, but we do have them all here. One or two of every sort you care to mention."

"A sort of Noah's Ark?"

"I'd say you have the idea. Of course it's ourselves that need a bit of support to keep going, as much as any of them, that's for sure. Just like the priest said." He gestured back towards the wards they had just visited. "However I don't think we'll be relying too much on what's coming out of the kitchen today to keep our spirits up, do you? We don't want you Dubliners thinking we can't look after ourselves down here. There's some good meat to be had from our own cattle on the farm over there, so I'll make sure a bit of the fillet comes your way."

Nights in the mental hospital were unexpectedly quiet after the bedlam of the day. Each evening, David, meal prepared, made plans to go into the town in the hope of meeting some of the local inhabitants. How else to avoid being caught in yet another ghetto? But what if he did encounter a girl? Invite her back to the asylum for a nightcap? She'd think he was a nutter. Instead he added a few more logs to the fire and lovingly prepared one of the fillet steaks that the farm manager himself had delivered. (The Chief had been as good as his word).

His grandmother Sabinsky, a name that had a ring of warrior status (Ivan Sabinsky Scabar) had rarely ventured out of her kitchen. Even the dining room, where his grandfather sat, seemed like it was in another country. Negotiations between the two parties were carried out by an emissary, usually their eldest daughter. More kugel or knaydlach in the chicken soup, or perhaps a second helping of kreplac? A man needs his nourishment. Dora, the stay at home daughter, an ambassador in all but name, kept the peace.

Besides, his childhood had trained him to make the best of his own company. TB and complications also breed isolation. What power. Just a small rod shaped organism. No flagella, can't even move by itself, never mind fly. In his sick-bed he'd played with toy soldiers, hanging Hitler whose pleas for mercy on the grounds of delusions of persecution were the cornerstone of his future interest in psychiatry. He'd given Adolph a fair trial. Through the window he could see his father as he practised his rifle skills, twice a day for the duration of the war. The target was the heart of a scarecrow with a black moustache, placed at the end of the garden.

Freshly crushed black pepper and a squeeze from a tube of Colman's mustard blended into the dark yellow butter —

another home produced item — then the problem of which wine he would select to accompany his meal. In deference to the Sabbath day, grated potato. Latkes instead of chips. Final few drops of the oil and vinegar dressing, a purchase from Rathgar, over a green salad; the last tie to the Dublin deli. After dinner he settled down by the fire with the remains of the bottle, his determination to join in the communal life of his new environment gripped by passivity. Little incentive to grasp that nettle. No longer the seventeen year old who had been driven by uncontainable desires to The Four Provinces or The Crystal Ballroom, hoping to find a princess in that seething mass of semi-sordid flesh. The object of his desire was not down town but there in Saint Elba's. Two weeks had passed and David, in spite of hovering about the entrance to the administration office whenever he dared, had not yet caught a glimpse of Deirdre Gillespie.

That afternoon's staff meeting, to which he had been invited, was attended by a select group who worked closely with the Chief. The presence of Father Fintan Dunbar surprised David, as did the warm handshake with which the priest greeted him.

Wilfred Behan stood in front of his team, He spoke in a serious voice, pausing only occasionally to sip from the large tumbler of water on the desk beside him.

His colleagues sat, engrossed by each item, as he gave advice on the problems left over from the previous day's work. To a question put to him by one of his audience who was uncertain about what treatment was appropriate for melancholia, he responded. "Remember, a patient's despair may be the handle he offers us to help him understand himself. Don't insult him by repudiating his pain."

As soon as his senior had sat down the Deputy head nurse, Declan Lynch, took over, the switch occurring almost indiscernibly. He reviewed, with equal gravitas, the list of concerns that had been passed to him from staff nurses on the wards. While the group followed each issue with a fervent concentration, David struggled to sustain attention to the mass of detail.

Don Juan's trump card was his matter o' fact approach but there was no way that he could see himself in Rhett Butler's shoes. His problem was that he did give a damn but was it insane to imagine that she might, or to believe that the one smile she had bestowed on him could have any real significance? But surely a stranger alone in a mental hospital was allowed to dream. He rested his head on the palms of both hands. *Has the fantasy of Deirdre Gillespie become more important than any action I might employ to involve her? Am I just another who has chosen to practice the arts of masterly inactivity, the Irish solution? Then again it might simply mean that the object of desire is unavailable, away on leave, and that is why I have not seen her. Sometimes the simple solution is the most convincing.*

Suddenly he became aware of the silence in the room.

"Like to tell us more about that listening cure of yours, Doc?" The Chief, who had sat down beside the priest, was smiling. "I don't blame you going off into your own world. I do the same thing myself, especially at these meetings where we must get through the more mundane tasks of the day. He laughed aloud. "It's hard to make tube-feeds or shock treatments sound appealing, although I try my best."

Now he turned away from David, who was still showing signs of embarrassment at being found lacking.

The Chief looked across to the priest for support. "It's not that we don't wish to hear more about what our patients are saying, is it, Father?" Fintan shook his head. "But it often seems like the last thing we are able to give time to."

"Oh, but we do try, Chief, and you get the credit for that." The Deputy Lynch looked over at Sarah, who nodded in agreement then folded her arms across her chest. The viola, having drawn its bow, could rest.

"Well I'm glad you both think so. What little we do achieve is a team effort." He hesitated, his voice sounding a little tired. "I'm sure you've noticed that. The pity of it is that we have to do our real business outside office hours." Wilfred Behan addressed his remarks directly to the locum. David felt that all eyes were now on him as the Chief continued, "And I can't say that we always have the knowledge or the skills we need when it comes to dealing with the darker side of our own emotions. Perhaps that is where you will be able to help us, Doctor? But I hope now you can agree with us that being able to realize one's own vulnerabilities is not a disability in our method of engagement."

"Well, you've caught me listening to my own voices, and I am relieved you can see there is a positive side to this. However, I'm a bit embarrassed to tell you what they are saying to me." David flushed.

It was the priest who spoke out. "Don't be worried, Doc! At least you're not ashamed to admit to your day dreaming, unlike some in your profession. Let's just say all of us here have the good fortune to realise that we are all in the same boat and need to help each other out. I hope you don't mind me including yourself in that. Come now," he went on, his eyes not leaving the Doctor's face for a moment, "we mustn't get carried away by talk of what we can't do. Declan's right to remind us that it is thanks to Wilfred that we do have our miniature private army here; those of us who do want to take things a bit further."

A bit further, indeed! My radar signals danger. Not a mention of our superintendent at this little collective. A rat pack dropping bits of Galtee cheese for me to sniff at so I'll do it their way. They seem so sure that I'll be a recruit to their side.

Wilfred Behan stood up to signal the end of the meeting. As they left, the priest again approached David. "I hope I'm not being impertinent, but I know from my own experience how hard it is when you are a stranger, especially in a place like this. We are all behind the same wall, yet it's easy to get cut off from each other, so maybe you'll agree to me popping in to see you in the near future." He looked at David. "Don't worry, I'll not be visiting on parish duties." He laughed. "No, Doc, It's more likely that I'd be coming to share a problem with you, as well as a jar, if that's okay."

But I do worry. Being chosen does have its problems.

A mild irritation began to invade David's good humour. In the open air again, he breathed deeply (his father had always been an advocate of clearing the lungs of impurities) glad to have escaped the somewhat suffocating atmosphere of the meeting.

Declan Lynch, carrying a batch of patient files under his arm, walked beside him. In looks he was a younger version of the Chief, wearing an identical style of faded Sunday-blue suit. He spoke in a voice that matched the melodious quality of his senior even if the timbre was pitched a mite higher. "There are some grand spots around here for you to visit when you have time off, so you only need to ask any of us for the low-down and we'll direct you to the best shebeens in the area."

"That sounds like a good idea, and thanks." David hesitated for a moment before venturing. "I'm going towards the office so I'll deliver those notes for you if you like."

A few moments later David entered the administration office, a messenger without a message. Deirdre Gillespie sat behind her desk chatting to the young man beside her. Undeterred, he headed in her direction.

"These are for you." He coughed. Her hair, clipped at the nape of her neck by a silver brooch, was drawn back from her face. She turned around towards him. *Christ, she is Ireland. Her colour, her clothes, never mind those eyes. No wonder I'm dreaming about her. Beauty must have its own dilemmas, like a singer's gift — the voice can becomes the master of the body and demands constant attention; its owner merely a caretaker of the talent; then why am I leaving without another word when I could just ask her to come out with me? It's certainly not to save myself for some frum little lady who swaps halcyon youth for a sheitel, hoping to be married off by nineteen, her sell-by date carefully tattooed on her mind.*

She was smiling at him just as she had done when he first arrived at the office.

"These case notes are not for me, Doctor Benn," Deirdre called after him as he backed away, "but it's nice seeing you again. Is your house comfortable?"

He was at the door. "Don't worry, I'll look after them." She brandished the files in the air.

David waved to the barman as he left the lounge bar of the Grand Hotel and stumbled past the green uniformed porter who held the door open for him. In the lobby, chandeliers reflected their light on Victorian inlaid mirrors accentuating rather than camouflaging the establishment's daytime shabbiness.

On the High Street, a row of men's outfitters, clothing stores clustered together, had their windows covered in a protective film of yellow cellophane. Last year's fashions hung awkwardly on wooden faced models.

No wonder the commercial travellers looked so depressed. I'm desperate for something to eat. Where's the bloody car park gone? I'm bursting with needs.

The accident occurred as he was negotiating a dark winding road inside the hospital grounds. David's head jerked back, thrusting him out of his brief stupor as the car went out of control. He tried to pull the steering wheel hard to one side but his manoeuvres didn't work; both he and the car rushed straight at a tree. He shut his eyes and prayed.

Yis ga dah. Yis... He recited kaddish, the prayer for the dead, in mourning for his own short life. Then he flung himself into the space in front of the passenger seat as the car slid towards the towering oak.

A Yid in a skid. Heading where? The gates aren't golden after all. Perhaps I've come to the wrong ones. He felt intense pain in the back of his neck before his head jerked forward, hitting the side panelling of the car as he blacked out.

"It's the psychiatrist from Dublin. Have you got a torch?"
"What for, for fuck sake, there's a full moon above." The

night nurse peered into the wrecked car. "It's that new locum. We'd better get a doctor."

"Poor bugger, look at that car, will you?"

"Run over to the infirmary, Michael, as quick as you can now. I'll stay here and keep an eye on him."

Sister Eileen Fahy, whom David recognised from the occasional appearances that she put in at Behan's afternoon gatherings, smiled down on her new acquisition. The infirmary was a miniature hospital that boasted facilities the County General would envy. Her especial pride was the small operating theatre where emergency surgery could be carried out, but in fact was never performed. Visiting consultants, the archdeacons of the medical establishment, from the County would call in, mainly to enjoy Sister Fahey's tea and cake, before going on a quick visit to the ward to arrange for the patient to be sent to their own hospital. Hand picked by their own kind, these consultants ensured the perpetuation of the species by selecting look alike versions of themselves (David diagnosed the phenomenon as a form of incest) to succeed them. Sister Fahy had a talent for making them feel important. "Are you well enough for a short visit, Doctor Benn?" Her smile broadened into a beam as she straightened the bedclothes and tidied up his bedside table. "Be careful how you reply."

"What is that dirty grin about, Sister? Can't you see I'm in a delicate state of health. Aren't you supposed to be making me better?" He lay back in his bed drawing the blankets closer to him. "Even the trees have it in for Dubliners around here."

"Oh, so it's the trees now!" A new voice made him blink and sit bolt upright. "No wonder I had such a job getting in to see you. It's easier to get a visit to someone in the padded cells, for Eileen Fahy has you well cossetted in here." Deirdre Gillespie stepped towards him and laid the forms she was carrying on the bed. "Am I seeing things?" David reached out towards the chair which Sister had put by his bedside as his visitor sat down. She examined him for signs of injury. "A sorry sight indeed, Doctor Benn. I never thought I'd be visiting you as a patient so soon after enrolling you to look after the sick."

"Maybe that's the only way I can get you to visit me," David whispered, sinking down in the bed. Of Sister Fahy there was no sign.

Deirdre pushed the forms she had brought nearer his right hand which he'd left outside the covers. "They say you psychiatrists are as mad as your patients and I'm beginning to agree."

"Well then, as mad people can say what they like, maybe I'll risk asking you the question I've had on my mind since I first saw you." Propped on one elbow, leaning towards her. "What keeps you at a place like this, I wonder? Don't think I'm being rude, just curiosity, it goes with a job like mine."

His visitor shifted her chair back from the bed. "Why wouldn't I want to work here? Anyway, I thought you psychiatrists could sort things out without cross-questioning your clients."

"Now I've made you angry. Forgive me, won't you, please? I'm not a shrink at this moment but a crumpled patient in need of comfort. Never mind, I've just enough strength to grant your wish before I die." He reached out for the papers, turned over the pages signing them as she instructed, then handed them back to her.

"Don't worry yourself, I'm not that delicate." She reached out and touched him on the shoulder. "And neither are you, Doctor Benn. You'll be up and about before long, I'm sure."

He smiled at her. "I will if you say so, that's for sure. Maybe we are drawn to this place for the same reasons. Could that be so?"

"It could, I'm sure. Take care now." She turned and left the ward with a wave to Sister Fahy who had been sitting half-hidden by the door of her office. When his visitor had gone the nurse came over to the bedside and straightened the covers once more. "She's a bonny lass alright. You're not the first to ask her that question either, Doctor Benn. Not that I was listening or anything." She lowered her voice to a whisper. "Her family are not just well off, they are very influential in these parts. Have no doubt about it, they will have fine plans set out for their daughter to marry one of the strutting young bucks from a rich clan like their own. They'll not take kindly to her going against their wishes." She leaned over her patient and helped him sit forward while she puffed up the pillows supporting his head. "Oh, the Gillespies are the big noises in Dargle all right, and it must be a shock for them to have their daughter, with her university education and her posh connections, up at Saint Elba's, even if she is working here and not a patient. Her brothers give her a hard time when she refuses to date their friends. Still Deirdre must be fairly confident that any of them are most unlikely to follow her through the gates of Saint Elba's. Don't they all have some relative or other in the asylum, posh or not, and they'll want to keep hush-hush about them." She patted David hand. "Some of her sort go off to Africa in search of a purpose, but that young lady has the sense to see that she can do as much for herself and for others by climbing the hill at the back of her own garden. That must be good news for the likes of yourself."

Home again, a T-bone steak lay waiting on the kitchen dresser, *Another martyr for auld Ireland, Another martyr for the cause. Are the Gillespies that different from the Rubinsteins when it comes down to the bone? Inside the Cambrassil Street Ghetto, the Hassim excluded the Orthodox who excluded the Progressives. Even in the land of the holy and the persecuted, the capacity for bigotry finds a breeding ground. Refugees from teffilin and sidelocks, escapees from the fringes of one tradition, establish their own fortress of differences. Meshuganah, Chaserae, Traiffe, Schichsa, Goy stage whispered (their own brand of racialism) barely hidden behind the curtains of the persecuted.*

A glass or two of claret later, the healing process seemed well on it's way. The remedial properties of fermented grapes seemed to have won the battle over the unspeakable consequences of his sinful acts. Eating blood red meat that had not been slaughtered under the eye of the Beth Din — *traiffe* — and having amorous intentions towards a goshki girl, had perhaps been overlooked by a God, who, no doubt, was kept fully occupied by the more heinous crimes being committed further afield. At least David hoped so.

Like much of Ireland's priesthood, Father Fintan Dunbar had taken his vows to please his mother. She had watched people raise their hats to her brother, Father Tom, and wanted them to raise their hats to her son as well. To see people in the street lower their eyes and ask Fintan for his blessing was to experience a wave of sensual satisfaction that was something more than a mother's pride.

It was late on a Friday afternoon when the farm tractor, carrying bales of hay to supplement the cattle fed, passed by the priest's dwelling. Fintan, on his way to visit the locum, had just set out from his comfortable four bedroomed residence. He waved to the driver, then paused for a moment, as he invariably did, to admire the rich expanse of farmland surrounding the dwelling, A silent prayer of thanks to the generous Lord for the good fortune that had brought him to Saint Elba's passed his lips in a whisper.

"You look surprised, Doctor. You didn't expect me, in spite of my promises, did you? Admit it now, confession is good for the soul!" The tall figure of the priest, framed in the doorway, looked down on the young resident and stooped his shoulders to reduce his advantage. (The potato famine had not diminished the average height of the men of Ireland any more than the locum's stature had been enhanced by his recent high protein diet).

"I'm in the habit of being surprised since I set foot in this place, Father. Come on inside to the kitchen, it's the best room in the house and where I spend most of my free time." David lit the gas for the kettle he had already filled in anticipation of his own supper, then turned towards his visitor. "You'll have a small one while the tea's brewing?"

The priest looked round the room, his pursed lips shaped in distain. "There's plenty of possibilities for improvement here, I'd say, Doctor Benn. They should be ashamed of themselves putting you in this house. It could do with a good lick of paint and some new furniture." He looked contemptuously at the well-worn easy chair by the fireside. "Good health to you, anyway." Fintan raised his glass but did not drink from it, continuing his inspection instead.

"Don't worry yourself too much, it's comfortable enough," David got up to fill the teapot and set it down on a table mat. He prided himself on his contempt for three-piece suites, ornate headboards on beds, avocado bathroom sets and for the people who hankered after such icons of convenience. Locums, like gipsies, needed freedom from such encumbrances. "The kettle whistles happily enough and from the what I've seen even the mice in here don't have too much to complain about." Collecting the tea-cups from the dresser he sat down again opposite his visitor. He relished the prospect of relating the priest's visit when he phoned his father. "Some out there enjoy running down hospitals of this kind, but which of us does not need asylum at some point in our lives."

Fintan Dunbar rose to his feet; without saying a word he moved across until he was standing beside the psychiatrist. "Not long after arriving here, Doctor, I knew that I'd come to somewhere special. With this place as my parish I discovered, for the first time in my life, that I had a real opportunity to get to grips with my own problems." His large hand pointed to David's face. "You look surprised at my saying this."

"Well, our afternoon meetings did make me think a bit." David hesitated. "I guessed something of the sort was being worked out between you all. I am interested, as you can see." He leaned to one side to dodge the shadow cast by Fintan's bulk.

"We all hoped that would be your reaction. Usually people of my calling are seen as the saviour of souls. The idea that their priest might himself be in need of help is not a popular one." He broke off looking across at David then drained his glass in one gulp and thrust it into David's hand. "Fill it up again, the tea can wait." Taking a generous swig from the replenished tumbler he sat back in his chair, his gaze still fixed on his host. "Perhaps it's because you are a stranger that I have the urge to confide in you. For those with needs like mine caution itself would be the real madness." He inclined forwards, speaking in a whisper. "It was Wilfred Behan who first saw through the camouflage of this cloak I walk about in. I suppose it was obvious to his trained eye that I needed help, but until then everybody ignored the fact. As long as I delivered the message I'd imbibed from Maynooth College my congregation were happy."

Both men looked up with a start at the sound of gentle knocking at the front door. As David stood up to answer it Nellie entered the room.

"Holy Mother of God." She crossed herself. "I'll be back another time." She flung the words over her shoulder as she made a quick exit, leaving the kitchen door ajar.

"My standing in this place will shoot up now that Nellie has seen you honour my house with your presence." David closed the door watching through the window as the inmate sped back towards Saint Ursula's ward without a backward glance.

"She's another, like myself, who makes good use of this place." The priest, serious again, continued. "Before I came here I'd arrived at a point where the true facts of life had become like rare curios, hard to come by and in need of careful looking after. In my case the tragedy was that I could not put my treasures on display and I learned to hide my new-found knowledge under this auld uniform they dress me up in. Here, in this sanctuary, I met people who had a different set of values." He stared hard into David's face trying to read his reactions to these revelations. "A psychiatrist must absorb and digest; an oven in which the pot cooks slowly keeping the lid shut until the dish is ready to be served. Our inspiration, Wilfred Behan, listens to the voices and visions that haunt the souls of inmates, and his staff, treating the detail as crystals that reflect a person's essence, instead of dismissing them as the meaningless ramblings of madmen." The doctor watched the beads of sweat settled on his visitor's forehead as the priest leaned across the table towards him. "Maybe you don't realise, Doctor, how rare a talent that is. His intervention in my life was as dramatic as it was direct, and it has given me the courage to use the same approach. Perhaps I'll soon be able to share more of all this with you. Confronting Old Harry has its dangers." He paused, drawing the back of his clenched hand across his brow. "Do I shock you, Doctor?"

"Let's top up these glasses — or maybe it should be tea?" David pointed to the neglected tea-pot. "It'll be getting cold by now."

"I think it's maybe you, Doctor, that's getting the cold feet."Again he pointed his hugh finger at the young man's face. "Don't fret; I can't blame you with me rushing in here and pouring out my troubles and I'd hardly set eyes on you. I suppose it's obvious to you that I'm not exactly refined in matters of the etiquette of emotional revelations but I'm convinced that there is a great power in straight-forward talk. I fancy that I can tell a man who shares that belief."

Replacing the pot, David reached again for the Jamesons but held on to the unopened bottle staring hard at the priest. "Well, Father, as a stranger I've had to learn not to take too much for granted. I'm sure you'll understand my reticence, but you've got me interested. Come to think about it, I've often wondered if the Church itself does act a bit like a mental hospital, nurturing people fantasies and cushioning them from the harsher facts of life?" Relenting, he opened the bottle and poured the priest another whiskey.

Fintan Dunbar smiled for a second then his features darkened as he scowled. "My own trouble is that the Church has created a fantasy world and forced me to live in it." As the big man subsided back into his chair he seemed to shrink in size. "Until I came to this place I was staggering about a bit like a feckin robot driven by what others expected of me." The two men sat facing each other in silence, before Fintan reached out and laid his hand on David's arm. "Forgive me, Doctor, you must feel that 1 have taken advantage of your hospitality."

The priest collapsed into a posture of hibernation. A black cloaked giant, eyes closed tight, lock-jawed now where he had been loose tongued. The psychiatrist had difficulty in discerning if his visitor was praying or shutting out his embarrassment at having exposed himself before a stranger. When he opened his eyes again he had regained his composure but his earlier exuberance was missing.

"You've done me a power of good. To tell the truth, I'm glad I've shared my feelings about Saint Elba's with someone who can appreciate its value and I'd say that you, surely, have the gist of my meaning. Perhaps I've added to that list of surprises you've already come to expect from this place." His voice was gradually regaining its resonance, like a small boy let out to play again after being called inside by mother.

"We never did get around to that cup of tea, now did we?" David lifted the pot from the table.

"There will be many other times, my friend, at least I hope so." He looked down, smiling as he departed. "Beannacht De ort."

Nellie Collins lay back on the bed, one of six, in the bright airy room she shared with selected long-term patients. The corner position, with windows on both sides of the ward, although barred, ensured an excellent view across the bye-ways of the hospital. Beside her was a neatly folded copy of last month's *Dargle Examiner* sent to her by a childhood friend who still lived next door to her old family home.

Seated in an easy chair placed in what Sister Fahy had called the pilot's position, Finoola Joyce kept watch. As darkness encroached on her visibility she leaned towards the window, tilting gradually forward like the hand of a clock till her face almost touched the glass. Suddenly, half rising to her feet, she shouted over to Nellie, who had dozed off on the bed. "There they go. The Chief, with Father Dunbar, and that Gillespie girl. Thick as thieves they are too." She stared in disbelief at her friend. "How can you lie there on your bed? Come and look, will you." Her voice reduced to a whisper as she peered out again into the fading light. "You can hardly see her in those black clothes she's wearing. They're heading to the Chief's house, same as last week. And the week before that."

Nellie sat up with a start. "Still, thank God for that Mister Behan. Where would this place be without him. It's he that looks after us. Reilly's always running off to the races or some meeting or other." She laughed. "Didn't the *Examiner* have a photograph of him at the Limerick races on their front page after he'd told the hospital committee that he was busy at a very-high-up conference, in Dublin, no less. The funny thing was that nobody seemed at all surprised at the discovery."

"Is it true the priest was over at that new doctor's house?" Finoola pushed back the edge of her head scarf, from her Veronica Lake coiffeur. "He's only a locum, isn't he?"

"Why shouldn't he visit?" Nellie was on her feet .

"Oh, nothing." The scarf had slipped back across Finoola's cheek. "I heard tell that the new fella's a Jewman, so what would he be wanting a priest for!"

Nellie turned away, muttering to herself. Living in a mental hospital had sharpened her ability to deal with unwanted contradictions. "All those big-wigs are the same, isn't that so? They are only in it for their own interests. Maybe it's for the best that they are seldom around, come to think of it."

From the ward below the sound of a single cold scream was followed by silence. Both women ignore the sound.

"You're right." Finoola sat back in her chair. "We are better off with them away out of it. Especially those nosey-parker councillors who seem to love coming here, riding on their expense accounts, so they have to make themselves seem interested. What's the use of them coming around asking us silly questions. Like what are the voices telling you now Nellie, my dear?"

A second cry cut the air. Crow-like it reverberated between the two women who waited in silence till its sound had travelled out though further yards of stone.

Sometimes the Chief would sit for hours beside Lily. Her cry had become a monitor of the Asylum's anguish. He wanted to enter the world of her pain. Its reverberations echoed the shared distress of all the inmates. He tried to put words to it when the staff group met. A screech? Repeated without expectation or tears. Timing more reliable than the town hall clock. It left all who heard it haunted by its ghostly horror. Later he came to know it was the cry of an abandoned child whose call was never answered, who went on crying knowing that no one would come. No expectations. A cry of no hope.

Finoola pursed her pale lips. She had moved her chair even closer to the glass. "You have to think up something quickly to interest them." She took out the powder compact her last boyfriend had given her and examined herself in its tiny mirror. "These bigwigs needed to have stuff to write down in the notes. It's my guess that half those men want you to tell them something dirty, like priests do in confession when they ask you, 'is that all he did to you?' sounding very disappointed. Respectability must be very boring if they come to a mental hospital for a cheap thrill."

Nellie raised her eyes to heaven. "Go on, what the devil did you say to them?" She poked a finger at her friend. "You're not going to tell me…"

…"You've guessed it, sure enough. Haven't you got more brains in your little finger than the lot of those grandees put together. Don't I often make up things to keep them excited, for it's a bit boring if everyone tells them that all they were thinking were sinful thoughts. No, I jazz it up a bit; like I used to tell the priest how me and my friends at school were always initiating young boys, taking their trousers down as a sort of forfeit and playing with their willies."

Nellie looked at her watch as the scream, on the third stroke of its ghostly message, passed through them once more. She checked her watch again and nodded. "That's it right enough. Always bang on time. They'll be coming in for tea down there, the whole gang of them. Aren't we are lucky to have this place between the few of us. If I was down there in that ward I'd be screaming too, only louder." She got back on her bed unfolding the *Examiner*, holding it up in front of her as though she was engrossed.

Finoola nodded and turned back to the window looking wistfully out into the gathering darkness. "Oh, and those men believed me. Wouldn't they swallow anything to excite themselves. As if we'd be interested in some little feicer's private parts. Sure, woman have more things to dream about: romantic beautiful stuff, not their old rubbish. A quick fuck and they think we are their slaves. Now that is real madness. Ejets, the lot of them, taken in by us fussing around them because we need the few miserable punts they bring home."

She threw back her head and laughed.

Nellie poked her nose out from behind her paper. "You're a right case, Finoola." She switched on the bedside light. "But I'd be lost without you. Sometimes I think that Lily down there is screaming for all of us. Always at tea time. It can get very lonely betimes and it's then I feel that I want to do away with myself. One hour can be like a year. On and on. It's those times you realise the place smells of dead cabbage." She folded the paper carefully not looking up at her friend.

"Come on now." Finoola had allowed herself to collapse back in to her chair and was silent for a few moments. "But I know what you mean, that's for certain. I often think of them all back home in our little house with its two acres. Not how poor it was, or those pigs of brothers of mine pawing at me, or my drunken oaf of a father storming in from the boozer and terrifying the life out of us children while he laid into my mother f-ing and blinding till he got his pants down and slobbered on top of that poor woman." She raised herself slowly out of the chair, giving one long look through the window before she pulled the curtains across. "No, but I do remember her telling us stories of her brothers who'd escaped to America and how she dreamed of them asking us to go out there and join them in sunny LA. Somehow or other she kept her pride and the few dollars they sent back to her were hidden away for that wonderful day in the future that would never come. Maybe our Lily down there never has anything good to dream about."

The two woman were silent for a while rocking back and forth in a keening motion until Finoola burst out again.

"And I remember me Ma baking soda bread with cakes and biscuits and singing to us. That was a very long time ago, Nellie, when we were just tots. The little grey home in the west, it was ... That's what me Ma would sing to us when we were put to bed at night." She looked again at her friend who had stopped rocking. "Ach, com'on witch cha now. Aren't we getting a bit serious, the two of us." She got up and stood by the bed leaning over till her face was beside the other woman's head. "Did I tell you what I said to the Bishop when he came around with Doctor Reilly, who was as usual all puffed up and showing off. And his pocket hanky dangling out as though it was his prick that was on display? The bishop asked me how I slept at night. 'Badly, your honour', I said. It was because I kept hearing the fiddler as he scraped away in the dead of night and I had an awful urge to leap out of bed and dance. I was a great jigger, you know, in the auld days."

Finoola threw back her head and laughed.

"Oh, I see, sez he, all serious. It must have been the devil that was after your soul. Why yes, your Grace, I said, that man is everywhere, I'm told. He comes in all sizes, just like our own kind, and he has a great big forked tail, long arms and hairy fingers, if you follow my meaning, sir? Indeed I do, my child, he's almost in tears by now, isn't the devil all over the place, God save us. Then they both went off eyeing each other and looking very pleased with themselves."

The keepers of the keys, their earnest lives enlivened by such encounters in crazy wards.

"You booked yourself in there and no mistake." Nellie, looking more cheerful, got up from her bed as two of their room-mates entered. "Maybe we're born to see things most of them don't even bother about."

She smiled over at Finoola as she got up to pull the curtains closed. "I'd keep quiet about seeing things in this establishment if I were you."

Gemma O'Brien nudged Doreen Jordan. The new arrivals, back from work, unbuttoned their white overalls. "If you worked in the laundry like we do you wouldn't have the time for all that gossip. We see enough dirty linen all day without making our own."

Early in their medical training undergraduates undergo a severe test of character, each of them being obliged to dissect a dead frog. The aim of the exercise is to expose the nerve that is hidden beneath the hapless creature's sinuous leg muscle. This tissue is then subjected to an electric current. The reaction of the deceased amphibian is significant on two counts. Firstly because, if successful, the limb which has been connected to a pointer will record the consequential muscular twitch on smoked black paper wrapped around a revolving drum. Secondly, the realization or failure of the exercise invariably leaves an indelible mark on the students future prospects as a medical practitioner.

Doctor O'Shea, the anaesthetist borrowed from the County General Hospital, who now checked the gas cylinders in preparation for the weekly session of electric shock treatments for depressed patients, was one such case. His continued interest in this treatment was undoubtedly related to his repeated failure as a student to get a response from the frog's leg. Moreover the recent introduction of an anaesthetic which modified the patient's physical reactions during this E.C.T. treatment, preventing many from breaking limbs, had left Dr O'Shea a disappointed man. The best he could hope for was a faint twitch of the *obicularis oris* muscle.

Nurses who had delivered their quota of leaden cargo from distant corners of the asylum in the early hours of a cold spring morning stood by their charges awaiting inspection. Outside a light mist hung like a blanket just above the ground.

At the stroke of nine Sister Eileen Fahy, handsome and freshly starched, swished into the treatment room, casting a trained eye along the line of beds. Their occupants lay motionless, strapped down by torpor. Briskly examining the charts clipped to the ends of each iron bedstead, the charge nurse made a brief entry in her own small notepad.

David Benn, his head heavy from the previous evening's claret — he'd arranged delivery of a generous supply from a local vintner — paced up and down in the corridor between beds. He avoided the gaze of the nurses who all looked expectantly in his direction.

Surely the miniscule act of pressing a little red button could not be misconstrued. It might, after all, transport these melancholic figures out of their inertia. Too bad about their memory loss — could be for the best — as far as I know.

Doctor O'Shea signalled for the first shock to be administered. And no doubt bring relief to all the staff.

"Are you ready, Dr Benn?" The anaesthetist sounded irritated. David pressed the button.

Two minutes later Sarah leaned over to stroke the brow of her patient, Mrs Dymphany Murphy, whose husband, seated comfortably in Casey's shop front boozer, hurried through his fourth pint as he basked in his own sorrow. The frown had disappeared from Dymphany's expression but she was not smiling. The nurse, looking up, caught the doctor's eye.

A simple act of molecular redistribution. Nothing more. Heaven in art whose father are.

The absence of Grand Mal seizures, while a disappointment to some, enabled the staff to treat as many as thirty patients at one 'sitting' but it was early afternoon when David stepped out of the infirmary. He caught sight of Wilfred Behan hurrying towards him.

"I was afraid I'd miss you, Doctor. Sister Fahy phoned me to say the treatments were finished. He slowed down to a walk, panting slightly. "I'm not a great runner, as you can see, but as I had the afternoon off I wanted to ask you to come over to my place for a quick drink with myself and a friend before you head home. I've got someone there that I'm sure you'll be happy to meet." He looked sideways at the young doctor. "ECT's not your favourite treatment, I'd say, but the Superintendent's sold on it. If you don't get a result with ten treatments, he tells us, just give another ten."

They entered the substantial dwelling set within sight of the locum's house. It was surrounded by a well kept garden and partially sheltered from view by large trees scattered here and there behind an established beech hedge. "Not your favourite either, by the sounds of it." David countered.

"Any more than deep insulin coma therapy. The fantasy of a second coming. Miraculous rebirth is a common fantasy in this country. Mercifully that particular treatment is going out of favour, for we've had quite a few deaths of the irreversible kind, on the D.I.C.T ward." The Chief hesitated. "To tell the truth, my personal views on these matters are that madness in all its forms frightens us into treatments which make little sense themselves. Doctors want to think there's a chemical cure for all human suffering, as they do in other branches of medicine, otherwise they feel out of their depth." The two men had entered through the front doorway when Wilfred turned to the locum.

"I hope you'll forgive me being so frank about your profession. I tend to rely a lot on my instinct, and it is telling me that there is no way you are that sort of medic." David shook his head. Nor, for the record, do I believe in leucotomies although I see they are still carried out at the General. He stopped, looking around him in surprise. "Why, entering your house is like stepping into a Spanish villa, Wilfred!"

The large circular hallway, painted white, curved its way upwards around three flights of winding staircase. Scattered here and there on the stained wooden floors lay well worn rugs, woven in wool, with Celtic designs — some dyed deep reds others of dark brown. The walls were bare except for one, from which narrow strips of tapestry depicting figures from Andalusian folklore hung in long lengths. Deirdre Gillespie emerged from the kitchen carrying a tray with glasses on it. "I have taken the bottle from its hiding place as instructed, so its in here waiting for us, gentlemen." She threw open the door of the vast sitting room and turned to David, who had followed her in. In this setting she looked like a Spanish gypsy woman, lips as full as the constrained breasts, wild horses bursting to be free from behind the roughly knitted sweater, mocking eyes teasing him beneath the red bandanna holding thick black hair from her face. So different from his image of her sitting in the administration office. Then, in spite of his preoccupation with Deirdre, his eyes were drawn to a small print hanging over the fireplace; apart from that picture the walls were bare. "Bernini", Wilfred volunteered, "The Ecstasy of Saint Teresa. Our last priest gave it to me."

"Poteen," Deirdre mimicked, pouring the spirit and handing out the glasses, "The Ecstasy of the Underworld. Still a state secret, I believe? Anyway, here's to the power of the Saints."

"And the sinners too," The Chief pointed towards a plate of sandwiches that were laid beside the tray. "Have a bite to eat first, Doc. You might just need a bit of lining for that drink since you've been hard at work all morning." Taking a mouthful from his own tumbler he gazed in admiration at the remaining poteen in his glass. His two guests followed his example. The Chief waited until they had sampled the white spirit, then turned to the couple who stood nervously side by side. "You've met already, I know, so no introductions are needed. People are drawn together by the same secret ingredients that bind the molecules of that potato juice you have in your hand so I'm suggesting you're both off out for a meal, later on, to find out if the chemistry works."

"You old matchmaker, I'd never have guessed you had it in you." Deirdre looked over at David. "He's a little different from some of the lads my mother tries to get me off with ... sort of paler, shorter, thinner and bit foreign about the face."

David took a gulp from his glass. *Sounds as though she likes me ... or is it the drink that makes me think so?* He rejoined. "You have looks enough for a regiment of monsters, so that should not put you off. As for me, seeing you out without your forms waiting to be signed confirms my first impressions. What are you doing here, I wonder?"

Deirdre stood up. "I'm afraid I have to be off now, but what do you say, Doctor, to meeting me at Corrigans, down by the quays. Saturday, at 2 o'clock if you can make it."

The two men watched as she prepared to leave putting the brown tweed jacket loosely around her shoulders.

"That drink has put new fire in me, you old hypnotist." Deirdre lent over to kiss the Chief's forehead. Waving at David she called back from the door. "Stay and have another glass of the punch. There's a lot Wilfred needs to say to you, that I know."

When the front door closed the nurse went over and pushed the sandwiches in front of David. "Have another of these and I'll top your glass up a little. Indeed, she's right, there is a lot to say but maybe most of it can wait awhile."

"You've done me a good turn there. I don't know how you found that out, but inviting me to your house and meeting Deirdre has certainly made me feel I'm no longer the stranger. Being a locum doesn't give one much time to settle in; I was getting anxious that my term here would be over before I'd got to know more about the country of my birthplace. Dublin isn't exactly the heart of Ireland, and even there I can't claim to have escaped the ghetto mentality of my race.

"I've a feeling that our whole country has slipped into a ghetto of its own, banning the books even if they don't actually burn them in the name of some kind of fanciful notion of a Celtic Twilight." The Chief let his guest out, watching him as he made his way a little unsteadily through the garden.

Are you ready for the road, Doctor?" The tall figure of the priest shepherded his companion towards the red Ford Anglia.

"I'm glad it's you driving, Fintan." David got into the front passenger seat and slammed the door shut, watching with interest as the cleric squeezed his bulk behind the wheel. "That slight altercation with the tree has made me think twice before I get into a car."

"You'll be safe as houses with me, David. After pouring out my troubles to you it's the least I can do to show you around this little town of ours." The priest chuckled. His Anglia, a winged horse. Both hands on the top of the wheel, the whites of his knuckles showing, he tooted the horn as they passed though the gates on to the main thoroughfare. "Wilfred and myself are of the opinion that being stuck up at the hospital is no life for a young fellow."

The road was deserted until they were in sight of Mulligan's.

That's what attracts the tourists, David's father would say. They come in their hordes to get away from the crowds.

A small group of men gathered outside the shebeen saluted the priest's car as it pulled on to the grass verge. Fintan bent his head to avoid the thick wooden beam above the entrance, standing by the bar as the landlord began pulling his pint of Guinness.

"The same for you, Sir?"

David nodded looking around the tiny room as they waited. The faint whirl of excitement that had greeted their arrival subsided as the men in collarless white shirts and black suits turned back to their glasses of stout. The drinks matched the colour scheme of the clothing like some new rendition of the national flag. An army of warriors who no longer listened for the call that might have made known their valour. The two men were left undisturbed at their small table, separated as though they were in a snug that was partitioned off from the other drinkers. Fintan took a deep gulp from his pint, holding the glass up for a moment in reverence to its creator before turning back to his companion. "That poor lad Christy, I thought he was a goner. Even the superintendent knew he had a weak heart, but I don't think anyone expected him to collapse like he did. And was it you that got to him first, Doc?"

"No, Sister was there already, busy dishing out the Spanish brandy. The heart had stopped beating altogether. I managed to get a syringe of adrenaline from the drugs cupboard and inject it straight into his ticker, so we already had our share of miracles when you arrived with your Holy water."

"By the look on your face when I dispensed God's message, I was sure it was you we'd be treating next!"

"I won't deny it, but tell me, Fintan, which of us is going to claim the credit for reviving the young fellow, and hauling him back from the arms of the angels?"

They stroked their chins, and sipping deep into the darkness of the Guinness shook their heads. "Is it a mystery of the Holy Trinity for the wise men of Maynooth College, or a clinical challenge to set before the College of Physicians? Let's hope the drug companies don't hear about it. For the moment at any rate." David hesitated. "I'll put my money on the Brandy."

The priest turned to Mr Mulligan.

"Two Remys, Sean, and a couple of pints to swill them down with." He grasped his hands behind his head and leaned back in the chair, lips pursed. "Don't we have some heavy thinking to do, and a modest bit of debauchery won't bring us to any harm. I'll still be able to forgive them their few venial sins when they come to confession." He tilted his glass a fraction to the company out of habit, but they were all now deeply engrossed in their own business. David washed the last drops of the brandy down with the Guinness. He congratulated himself on his foresight. With his manhood on the line he had made sure to eat a good meal before they had set off. His father had prepared him well for the rigorous tests of integration.

An hour later the pair left Mulligan's to head into town. The neon lights of Dargle drew a more glamorous clientele into the city centre as it attempted, with due modesty, to emulate the night life of Dublin. Released for the evening from the drab surroundings of the hospital the two men were determined to enjoy their outing together. They walked side by side along Dermuid Street, past the queues for the last performance at the Savoy Cinema. Neon lights illuminating the signboard. Coming soon....

Beauty and the Beast. *If you believed that you'd believe anything. What's on the way is a cut to pieces version of some innocuous story. Their fairy tale is of eternal life, walking on water, confession with absolution. Grace Kelly, to make it believable, all at an inclusive price; your sense of reality. But who cares when our Kelly's daughter is looking down on us from the hoardings. Such a tasty dish and ready to melt the hearts of the innocents as well as the doubters for only half a crown. A value bet as they say in Kilmartins.*

They decided against going to the Grand Hotel choosing instead to call in on old established, but recently refurbished, Gregory's Hotel and lounge bar.

"Will you look at that, David, God's creatures in all their finery." At the entrance to the lounge bar the priest sighed deeply. His speech slightly slurred, he stood for a moment hand on chest, both eyes closed in homage. "Those mini-skirts must have been invented in heaven. Thighs are the highway to paradise, without a doubt. Let's hope the angels run out of fig leaves. I suppose they'll call it The Revelations."

"But for whose benefit, I wonder?" David raised his eyes to the heavens. "I hear it's full of old men up there in the clouds. Maybe they make the rules to suit themselves."

No divorce, no contraception, eternal damnation or England if you want a job or an abortion. "I can't argue with that." The priest laughed. "You Dubliners have a direct line to the beyond, I'm told."

"And to the other place down below." David moved towards the bar. "It's my round now, so sit quiet there before you get into trouble. Listen to the music and I'll fetch the poison."

The singer's voice was only just audible above the hum of fervent revelry.

"At the Cork exhibition there was a young lady
whose fortune exceeded a million or more
But a poor constitution had ruined her completely
and medical treatment had failed o'er and o'er."

"So you learned Irish at Trinity College did you?" The priest faced his companion across the table, the replenished pint in his hand. "If that's not a contradiction, what is!"

"Do you mean that I've no right to be interested in learning the language of the country I'm born in?"

Compulsory Irish was taught at Zion schools. Hebrew was voluntary.

Fintan drained half the contents of his glass before slamming it down on the table in front of him. "Come now, I expect you have a reason for saying that, but for God's sake, you surely don't suspect me of such ideas? No, I'm trying to tell you that, having been brought up on Gaelic myself, I can barely find an occasion to use it. The tragedy for me, dear Doctor, is not surrendering our language, it's losing our people." He fidgeted.

Jews do this when they see one of their own on the other side of the barbed wire.

Shrugging off his discomfort the priest offered an olive branch. "Maybe you've a reason all right," he suggested, "for this country does lack a soul since we opted out of the war against fascism. Not that you'd expect us to line up with the English."

"Give over your doctors and medical treatment
I'd rather one squeeze from the bauld Taddy Quill"

The singer droned on, ignoring the hubbub of chattering *hoi polloi* who crowded into the bar.

For a while Fintan seemed to be listening to her intently; then leaned over and murmured: "There are Irishmen across in London that are ashamed to be spoken to in their own language.

Maybe they share your ideas for I've heard they think they are being talked down to. Did you know that, a cara?" The priest sighed. "A sad thing all the same when a country loses its self respect." He looked up to see that David had turned away to applaud the singer. The priest drained his few remaining drops of beer and waved the glass around. "De Valera, you know, Doc, seemed to believe like Ghandi, that modernization leads to loss of national identity. Isn't that 'bollocks'. I'd say it was just a cover up for the fact that he'd lost the plot! Caught between the devil and the deep blue sea, poor bugger." Fintan looked around the room. "Even the music in this place is stuck in the past. I'd rather hear Sargent William Pepper than The Old Bog Road. It's nineteen sixty nine, not nineteen sixteen after all!"

"How are you, Father, it's good to see you in such high spirits. Is it a sermon you're delivering or what?" The man who stumbled up to the priest, his smiling countenance, a cross between a bank manager and a prosperous farmer, scanned the faces of the two men for acknowledgment of his whimsy. His quizzical gaze settled a moment too long on David.

"But I have not come to interrupt your drinking. I've got a tip for you, Father, and for your friend here. Now the interloper, his smile broadening as he stared more intently at David, lowered his voice to a whisper. "Your people", he confided, his smile unremitting, "have a great interest in the old nags, just as we do. Am I right?" A deep breath puffed his chest out. "Well, I have a wee tip for you both. Look out for Bantry Bay when she runs at Tralee. She's a bit special, so don't miss it whatever you do. A few punts on the nose won't go astray. A bit special, so keep it to yourselves," he repeated, waving over to some friends at the other end of the bar as he turned to leave, "God bless you both."

When he had gone Fintan turned to his friend, his mood more serious. "*Your people* is it? Maybe he thinks I'm Father Creagh and we're back in nineteen hundred and four?" The priest scowled, muttering to himself "talking like that in front of me as though we are back in the dark ages."

The priest sighed loudly as his companion looked at him in surprise. "Oh yes, I am acquainted with the Limerick pogrom." He reached into his pocket for a cigarette then glancing up at his companion he put the packet of Gold Flake unopened down on the table. "Anyway, come on now, or we'll both be needing ECT; none of this will stop us having a flutter on that nag, will it now? Bye the way, I heard on the grapevine that you're keen on our Deirdre Gillespie. She's some woman all right!" He took another close look at David as he spoke, "And she has a mind of her own. Taking shelter with us is hardly the hippie alternative life style."

"Not much that escapes your eye, Fintan." David raised his voice as some of the clientele began to join in the singing. He moved his chair closer to Fintan. "Anyway, my friend, you're not too far of the mark there. She's not your usual trendy, by any stretch, is she? I'd never have dreamed I would have any chance of interesting her, what with all those brawny stallions she has to choose from, but maybe, for once, luck is on my side and the differences are in my favour rather than the reverse."

"That's more like it, man. You certainly do bring something fresh into our midst, David. Wasn't it Joyce himself that said there was no anti-Semitism in our little country?"

"No Jews, no anti-Semitism, is what he said!" David shouted.

The priest looked at him seriously. "Have you considered that the very difference that so engages you is what encourages our little group to take you into their confidence so perhaps being the locum has some advantages after all. Sort of speeds things up. Does that surprise you?" The priest gripped the young doctor's arm. "Maybe you haven't yet cottoned on to the fact that we are needing your help fairly urgently."

"Is that why Deirdre has agreed to come out with me?" David felt a chill of disappointment.

"Didn't you, yourself, say that she has a mind of her own? I can assure you, that *is* the case. Just be careful you don't tread on the toes of her family. The Gillespies are a force to be reckoned with in this town. I could tell you a tale or two about what happens when they are crossed." Fintan hesitated then leaned over closer to David and whispered loudly. "But don't worry yourself too much about that now, Deirdre will take care of them." He lowered his voice to a whisper. "It's me that's the cause of all the worry. When I tell you the full story you'll have some idea as to why we need your help." He picked up his glass. "Come on now, we'll finish these drinks, then I think it's time that we two were heading back."

The priest hauled himself to his feet, knocking against the table as he did so. "Not much room for a full size man here, is there?" He pushed his chair aside with his foot. "Let's be off now. Back behind the wall for us both, and maybe a small nightcap as a reward for good driving." Moving quickly ahead of Fintan, David held the door open as his friend staggered out. "Don't worry about a thing Doc, this car is as docile as a tame donkey; it'll carry us back home, no trouble at all."

Our wills and fates do so contrary run
That our devices still are overthrown,
Our thoughts are ours, their ends none of our own.

The Player King in *Hamlet*

"Can I get you some tea, gentlemen?" The patient trembled with the anticipation of pleasuring his visitors. "Two sugars, Doctor Benn?" He bowed. "None for you, Mister Behan." His faded gentility suggested that deep beneath the courtesies it was he, Victor Graham Wilson, who was running the show. "I'll bring it along to you shortly with a few of the cream crackers that my wife brought in."

"Thank you, Victor," smiled Wilfred Behan. David smiled too, trying not to flash knowing messages to the Chief. Once inside the office he could restrain himself no longer. "Could be a hotel manager welcoming his week-end guests?"

"Hard to believe he was close to death's door a few weeks ago."

The nurse sat back in the comfortable arm chair. "This ward creates its own illusions. Doctor Reilly's shop front, the Imperial Hotel of our asylum. Some of his rich private clients are admitted here."

Saint Ignatious ward was situated near the entrance to the hospital grounds, shaded from view by a bodyguard of ornate shrubs and flowers. Visitors were spared a journey through the grounds and perhaps a confrontation spared some of the more disturbing consequences of chronic mental illness. It rivalled with the Infirmary for the prize of the most extensively refurbished unit. 'O'Dearest' mattresses on every bed. Herein lay something of a paradox: over-protection from the facts of life was thought by many experts in the art of child rearing to leave its victims vulnerable to mental breakdown.

Having serviced his visitors Victor waited patiently outside their office while the two men discussed his problems.

"I'm glad you are here, Doctor, for Victor's case has me enthralled. First I'll fill you in on this man's history." The Chief flicked quickly through the case notes then put them abruptly to one side. He had already absorbed each nuance of the patient's fabrication.

Since arriving at Saint Elba's, over a decade ago, Wilfred had set himself the task of understanding the ways of madness in all its guises. His first priority had been to improve the lot of the psychotic inmates. To achieve this he'd set up groups for the nurses and given them permission to talk about their own emotions. In this endeavour he'd met with opposition from some (*We're not the fucking inmates; we're the staff*) while others blossomed when they saw how this freed them to get closer to their charges.

Sarah had volunteered "When I was a kid I had nightmares, strange shadows, falling into space, being pursued by dragons; they all felt so real, I thought I might never wake up." All the while he'd kept an eye open for cases, such as Victor's, who he might rescue from the nemesis of the Superintendent's fast-delivery remedies. They provided him with a different kind of challenge. Victor Wilson was a case to be rescued, a case to illustrate the dynamics of conflict which could be more easily engaged with by staff. More accessible than the chronic psychotics and perhaps less threatening.

"Here is someone who has created himself in the image of how he thinks people want him to be." Wilfred took the patient's file from the desk and handed it to David. "A skilled juggler who can skip in step with the tune that others play. Fred Astaire might envy him; tap dancing to our music, always in harmony with what he sees as our needs." The nurse, warming to his task, groped for another metaphor. "A tight rope artist who seems like the perfect partner." He grinned. "Enjoy that cup of tea, he's brought in his own selection of blends imported from the foothills of far off Assam, for our delectation."

David sipped from his mug and nodded his satisfaction as the Chief continued.

"No delusions, except for his obsession. A successful banker who lives in the best part of town. Near Deirdre Gillespie's parents, in fact. Three weeks ago he attempted suicide and was admitted to hospital. He waited in silence until David had read the file. When the psychiatrist had finished, the Chief leaned across the desk to whisper: "I come to talk with him each day." He hesitated, then registering David's approval, added: "I shouldn't say this, but Victor reminds me a bit of my deputy, Declan Lynch."

"I see that Doctor Reilly wanted him to have shock treatment to cure his depression." David pointed to the scrawled insert in the notes. "Yes, and tranquillisers when he gets high again."

The nurse frowned. "I know these measures are necessary sometimes but he makes no attempt whatever to help this unfortunate patient understand what kind of anxiety drives his strange behaviour.

"Perhaps there is nothing but his obsessions behind his character? Anyway let's have him in and hear what he has to say."

"That's his fear, Doctor, that's his fear. He's like a child who followed the Pied Piper into another world and has never grown up. He woos us now the way he wooed his mother. Seducing her with a heady cocktail. She seemed to have forgotten that a child must bite the hand that feeds it in order to release itself from the ties of love."

"My rebellion was to wear two different coloured shoes." David said sadly. "And yours?"

"Reading books when I should have been out in the fields helping with the harvest."

"Not exactly Che Guevaras are we?" The two men shook their heads in sorrow. "We'd better have the patient in now. Maybe I can help you, Wilfred, to find out if he has a secret hidden self. If we succeed in discovering it we must show this poor wretch that we are interested in that, rather than these exotic tea-leaves he has used to charm us."

Victor Wilson seated himself nervously in the easy chair smiling at the two men without actually looking directly at them.

"Your tea was delicious, Victor." David raised his cup. "But share with us the details of what deflates you and leaves you feeling so down? Who pricked your balloon this time to transport you to such a point of despair? Your wife, your cleaning lady, the postman?"

After a long silence Victor turned towards the Chief. "I think the Doctor here is trying to get at the same point that you made to me during our talks." He had gone pale. His skin clammy with perspiration. "How can I tell you? Something so small, it would seem of no consequence to others. My wife was in bad humour over a trifling matter, a cake that failed to rise, I think. It had nothing to do with me, but she blamed me when the sponge was flat. Maybe I slammed a door at the wrong moment?" He grimaced, staring forlornly first at one and then the other of his therapists. "A man of your race, Doctor Benn, must truly scorn my petty burden."

"Ah, but when you felt you have sacrificed your whole identity to make things right for her, not having it appreciated was devastating for you." David grimaced but side-stepped Victor's comment on his origins. It was hard to know if he was trying to ingratiate himself or hitting back.

The patient nodded looking down at the floor before speaking. "I do have my own life, but I've hidden it away. You are right to say that nobody realises how much that has cost me. Dancing to attend to them, pondering how I can surprise them, and for what? To be kicked in the teeth? At night I dream of things I'm ashamed to confess to. I comfort myself that way until I drop off to sleep. As a child, knowing my mother disapproved of any show of emotion I tried to find a new life for myself. I'd get off the bus on my way home from school and spend a half hour, the same amount of time every day to dispel her suspicions, wandering around mostly in a daydream of what I might do or where I might visit if I could run away from home. Then, as I got older, I began to have sexual fantasies. I'd buy a film magazine and pour over their glossy pages full of beautiful actresses. The half hour gone, I'd shove it in the nearest waste paper bin before getting home. Lana Turner in her best dress squashed up with the remains of someone's cold fish and chips." He sobbed quietly, his childhood bartered into slavery, never to be reclaimed. "I was not like other boys who share their thoughts with school pals. Most of my time was spent at home trying to pleasing mother. How could I have any close friends?"

"But you got plenty of thrills from sucking up to mother." Behan volunteered gently.

"That is true. She preferred me to the rest of our family putting me ahead of both my father and my brother who was four years older than me. My addiction, I suppose." He turned to Wilfred. You've helped me understand that. Not so much my mother's needs, perhaps, as my own unwillingness to share the prize with my father and brother. I'm getting the message." As he got up to leave he smiled at David. "I've heard of people who look in dustbins to find out things about their owner's private lives. Garbologists, I believe they are called. Well, maybe I'll try looking for some of my lost self in the same quarters." He bowed slightly. "Thank you, Chief, and you too, Doctor, for showing an interest in me." The office door had hardly closed behind him when it opened again as he popped his head around it.

"Either of you like another cup of Assam?"

He didn't wait for their reply but they heard him chuckle from the other side.

Corrigan Limited, a one time shebeen of Number 2 The Lanes, now double barreled and renovated to retain its seedy mystery for the new clientele who had none of their own. A poster of Bogart puffing on his cigarette at Rick's Cafe in Casablanca hung above a faded no smoking sign. Sam had lost his job to Hoagie as Old Buttermilk Sky honky-tonked from a hidden recess of the bar. David sought a corner table by the window, his own position partially concealed by the flamboyant swathe of material that hung from the curtain-rail. Settled in his crow's nest, he carefully unfolded his copy of the Irish Times. One brief glance at the headline before he turned to study the runners on that afternoon's Mallow race card. Deirdre was already inside the bar, chatting to a group of young men seated at a table by the door, when he spied her. He saw them look over in his direction.

As she approached him David lowered his paper and nudged the chair opposite him back from the table for her to sit on. Dressed in a double breasted grey linen jacket and skirt, the Spanish gypsy was nowhere to be seen. Perhaps she'd just been to visit her parents. The priest had already warned him that they liked to call the tune.

"There should be a poster of you up on the wall beside Bogart, for you'd knock spots off those Hollywood beauties."

"Come on, I've enough of that sort of rubbish from those eejits over there." She nodded across to young men who were making a noisy exit. "Tell me how your injuries are coming along."

So she knows. I bet her friends warned her off me. Did they call me a bloodsucker I wonder?

David held up both hands. "I'm glad you asked. In fact I was not sure you did realize that Jews drank the blood of Christian children." He leered across to where Deirdre's friends had been sitting. "Ask them. They know all about it. Probably learnt it as part of religious education at school."

Deirdre raised her eyes to heaven.

"Rest assured that the sacrifice is in a good cause. All that blood we lose at circumcision has got to be replenished somehow." He shrugged. "You'll understand. Beggars can't be choosers. Our supplies come from the bodies of murdered gentile children. Be sure, we do have standards. Not like those vampires who drink from sleeping beauties in the dead of night. Surprised, are you? Maybe you haven't noticed it happening? That's because we mix the blood with our matzo meal to disguise the terrible deed."

Deirdre leaned forward and examined David closely. "It's just as well I didn't introduce you to that mob. What would I say? You're not quite us, but you're not quite like them either. They think your lot all go round in black coats with dreadlocks under your hats."

"*Rugadh in Eirinn me.* Born and bred in this country. My own grandparents were drawn to these shores by some mysterious force. Rumour has it that they set off from Russia to get to New York. Maybe God in his wisdom was arranging a shiddach between the two of us." David shook his head sadly. "The truth is, Deirdre, that I'm no longer so sure that you can be Irish and Jewish at the same time. Could be what I've come here to find out."

"It looks like that accident has left a permanent scar." She reached out a hand and stroked his head.

Deirdre banged her empty glass down on the table and pointed to David's newspaper, open at the racing page. "Come on, let's get out of here, we can just make it to Mallow if we leave now. It's getting a bit stuffy in here." She hauled David to his feet. "Horses aren't into racialism, as far as I know."

"You direct me and I'll pick a few winners in return. How's that for a deal?" David lowered the hood of the small sports car he had rented, then held the door open for his companion. "Isn't this the jazzy number, Deirdre, all done to impress yourself."

"I'll be impressed if you keep this thing on the road. The directions are no problem, but I have my doubts about your side of the deal." She reached into the back seat for the *Irish Times*. "Do you call this a racing paper?"

"Like myself, it has its moments. They actually gave a winner last week, and at ten to one. Mind you, the owner and the trainer were Prodies. Trying to help increase their readership to beat the Catholic rags, I suppose."

"Hadn't you better keep those thoughts for when you're safely back behind the asylum walls?"

They parked by the side of the road and walked together to the course. A man who seemed to have no legs, unless he had tucked them up under his body, begged for alms. He was getting what he seemed to be expecting; zilch, if his empty cap was anything to go by. Being legless did not seem to bother him unduly. *Drunk on self pity.*

Deirdre guided David through hoards of six foot high farmers who thronged together like some family of giants on a day outing. Past the beer tents and an assortment of musicians. Every now and then she exchanged a brief greeting with someone in the crowd, but did not stop to chat.

From the list of runners on the form sheet they made their tentative choice, then hurried to the parade ring to examine its credentials more closely.

"If that horse wins the jockey is going to have to carry it around." Deirdre pointed to a ragged animal who looked as if he'd been pulling a tractor rather than training for a race. "Of course, that's the one the form guide recommends. Perhaps we should try a new strategy — like tossing a coin?"

He took her hand, casually, to control his excitement, as they hurried to execute their new plan. In the stands they cheered with the rest of the crowd, straining to see their selection. A battle to the finishing post.

Horse racing was a key activity in Ireland's struggle with its depression. Being forced to eat potatoes to survive had left a scar in the nations psyche. Each race a little war of its own, a battle against the fates. Sir Ivor and Lester Piggott, living Gods who could be worshipped. Vincent O'Brien a warrior. Their deeds raised the nations flagging spirits.

A great cry went up whenever a horse crossed the line. Each winning jockey returned a hero, hailed by a beaming owner and surprised trainer. Losers were condemned out of hand as either useless no hopers, or bent villains who had deliberately thrown the race. The mountain of losing tickets, thrown to the ground in despair, grew as the afternoon wore on.

"Come on, David!" She put her arm around him. He pretended that her action was nothing out of the ordinary. "In the end I don't suppose it matters all that much. If you lose it's only what you expected. How else would the poor bookies pay for their stretch limousines. Tralee is the big one. What do you say?"

"I'll be driving more carefully from now on. We'll have a cup of tea and let the rabble rush home. There's a mountain of forward planning to do."

"You'll have to wait for me, anyway, while I collect on this little secret bet I sneaked on the Tote. 'Throwaway' at ten to one for a place." She waved her ticket in front of him. "Don't the women have it over you poor creatures, and no mistake."

Just before he dropped her off, David leaned back in his seat staring straight ahead. He tried to keep his voice casual, not wanting to spoil the first day they had spent together. "Is there some underground agenda at the hospital that I'm not privy to?"

She smiled at him but said nothing. "I feel I'm being given some special treatment," he hesitated, "as though I'm being assessed for a secret undertaking."

"One minute you are complaining that you feel out in the cold, the next that you're seduced inside. Try not to worry so much, I'm sure it will all become clear before long."

"Sure. With you beside me I don't really care, but," frowning again, "how do I know if you or the priest or even Wilfred for that matter are being nice to me for myself or for some imaginary skill you think I've got?"

Deirdre opened the car door then turned to David "You're an incurable case. I'm off now but I hope to see you again very soon." She kissed him briefly as she stepped on to the pavement.

Just one more kiss, Deirdre, by way of inspiration for the next meeting.

She waved back at him as she reached the turn in the road.

"*Glory Hallelujah, praise be to the Lord and to Hell with the Devil.*" *A miracle requires gratitude.*

That night he rang his father and told him how things were going.

"The Priest did you say, son? That's a bit of a coup, but don't get carried away."

"You know me better than that, Dad. The trouble is they don't understand down here that if a Jew's not worried there is something wrong."

"Yis go dah Ve yis go dah Sha may ra bah". David stood, hat on head, in the small synagogue that was nothing more than the drawing room of a modest terraced house on Drabmol Street near the centre of Dargle, reciting Kaddish in memory of his dead mother. Apart from the mezuzah on the door there were no external ways of identifying the role of the house. Chaim Hertzog's dwelling on South Circular Road was not that dissimilar.

No sounds from the neighbours, but could that mean they are listening in? These smells bring it all back.

Not being able to afford a regular Chazzen, the service was conducted by Mr Goldstein, a lawyer who returned to his home town to practise after a short time working as a trainee in London for an international law firm. His sermon, an incantation inviting the congregation of ten men and two women to return to the Promised Land.

Is that the battle I should be fighting? Proper guns and real arms. But as the sermon proceeded it became clear that the Promised Land was not the Palestine of today, where a bitter war was being fought in the shadow of holocaust memories, but a biblical vision of a place where the wandering Jew could settle in peace, sheltered under the wings of angels.

Mr Winestein, the shammes, moved from his front row seat towards the linen cupboard which was acting as an ark; always a modest piece of religious furniture which reminded the Israelites of their humble origins. He removed the Torah scrolls and held them in his arms while the congregation prayed.

There they go. The Holy Joes, smelling of mothballs and used black engine oil, demonstrating their dexterity. Anything you can do I can do better. No you can't. "Boruch atah adownoi...". The congregation muttered their responses to Mr Goldstein's prayers.

Yes they can, yes they can .... Little here for the earthly soul. They've learned their lines too well, and too soon. No trace of God in these rituals. Perhaps this is how true faith works, like those Canadian troops following orders on D Day. Here's not to reason why, here's but to do and die.......... Why has nobody talked to me? They must know I am a stranger in their midst. Perhaps, like the barman at the Grand, they think I belong behind the walls up there on the hill.

These places are like Wilhelm Reich's orgone boxes, releasing memories. Reminding us of the feelings that everyday preoccupations push out? Back to the 'nameless dread'......... Go on, give if a name, spell it out in a verse. Even the big shots here know that some day their name will be read out in the Kaddish service. The battle between the problems of facing one's own destiny and what is going to win the three thirty at Naas.

That old suffocating feeling taking over. Stifling with its sweet musty smell. It's not only the room that is small. A wandering Hebrew, unrecognized by Jews gathered in worship. A little clique, so enthralled by their mitzvahs and their dovening skills, that they cannot see the stranger in their midst. Vos machstu?

Could this happen if the Messiah dropped in for a cup of tea or a glass of holy wine? He'd do better in the Outer Hebrides or Inishbofin. What sort of ailment is this? Mr Goldstein has returned the scrolls to their resting place and walks back to his seat, head slightly bowed.

Nothing a good walk won't remedy. Plenty of fresh air the Doctor recommended for my childhood disease. Is that old Tubercular Bacillus invading ·the present? The locust hidden in the milk had arrived on a float, driven door to door by a donkey, and dispensed from an iron tank with a shiny brass tap. Good morning, Mrs Benn. Natural ingredients if ever you saw them. Blessed be the fruits of the earth. Like the stuff they are chanting here. Purity itself giving me the itch.

Delicate and prone to complications. The Proust of Mount August, Lower Kimmage Road and Terenure. One of the Jews kept waiting outside in the playground during their prayers. Was it the secret of the Kings clothing they were concealing from the enemy?

My childhood — eat your heart out, Gorki — living in the valley of death, walled off by suitcases, packed and ready for the journey on the already overcrowded Tubercular train to heaven. Having my own private bed with all home comforts was better than being sent to the sanatorium but even a mother's love can't erase the Reaper's kisses.

David walked back towards Saint Elba's. No one had spoken to him at the synagogue.

"Every Jew is bound by the Divine Command to love his neighbour as he loves himself, as it is written."

He waved to a young woman as she passed him.

"Thou shalt not hate thy brother in thy heart. He who hates a fellow Jew in his heart is guilty of violating God's Law, for it is written," (Leviticus 19:17):

"You seem preoccupied today, Doctor." She smiled. "I'm off to see my mother and to bring back some of her special fruitcake. It's the best in the County. They let me out occasionally so that I can stock up. I'll give you a piece sometime."

"Sarah, I'll look forward to that treat." David called after her as he passed through the gates of his new home.

Glad to be back.

It was a spring evening in Dargle. For some, the wheel of hope turned to try again. David and Deirdre had just set out for an evening meal in town. In a far corner of the hospital overlooking the abattoir, a part not blessed by the name of a Saint, Sister Fallon, whose life did not have seasons, put the finishing touches to the back of a Fair Isle cardigan. Forty years on the chronic wards, she could claim to know what each sound penetrating her office meant. Most could be ignored: mutterings of the chronic demented. 0-ward, as it was called by the few who mentioned it, had no visitors. Even the Chief had no authority to disturb the status quo. Sister's reports satisfied a management committee unwilling, themselves, to enter the snake pit. Of course, law demanded and must be satisfied. The official 'inspection' took place in sister's office twice a year. Her authority rested on everyone's knowledge of her indispensability. Nobody else was willing to spend time there, yet alone look after the pitiful inhabitants.

Tonight had been no different from any other. Now, Sister knew, from the hurried step of her assistant, and first cousin, that trouble was in the air.

Martha Murphy, after fourteen attempts, had succeeded in releasing her soul from its misery. By a planned act of self-abuse, Martha had achieved what all other forms of treatment had failed to do. She had discharged her tormented soul from this earth. Too long in the backwaters of the asylum, she had suffered the voices which whispered accusations in her ear. Nobody had ever entered her world to question these charges. Only Sister Fallon was there to housekeep. As for her fellow inmates? They too waited, unheard. Soon all would die out and make way for others in a more enlightened world. In this brave new era delusions and hallucinations would be seized on as handles to understanding. The Chief had read the works of the few: a psychoanalyst or two, a trio of revolutionary existentialists — all from across the water. They'd thrown away their doctors' uniforms.

Now the nurse walked unhurried to the ward and looked down at the slight figure of her patient, curled up in the bed. Too cold. The deceased had probably overdosed on sleeping tablets hoarded over a period of time.

She and her assistant said a brief prayer over the body before drawing screens around the bed. No one in the ward paid any attention to the proceedings. In the morning Sister would inform Doctor Reilly that her patient had died during the night. The superintendent would arrange for the GP on duty to write the certificate. Nobody wanted the suicide figures for a country who exported a large percentage of its healthy population to be magnified in the eyes of the rest of the civilized world.

David and Deirdre sat opposite each other at a corner table of The Abbey Tavern, Dargles lobster bar. Jammets of the south. Beige, brown and white, the tricolored banner of a subdued elegance that excluded any garish flavours. Whiskey sauce that complemented rather than polluted the native flavours of the lobster's noble sea tastes. The Head Waiter looked only at Deirdre when making his routine enquiries as to their state of contentment. His accent, an uncertain mixture of Spanish and American, did not disguise the banality of his style.

"Señorita Gillespie, your a beauty, its za daazzles me. If I may say so." David mimicked, reaching out across the table.

"Señor Ben-ne." She took his hand.

They ordered beef cooked in Guinness, eating it in silence.

Stuff the gaps: engulf my real appetite. Does not seem to have worked as it does for some. Those priests, cosseted with good food and drink. They fill up with breakfast, the works, including pig's blood, fried eggs and faggots, God save us. Then lunch, afternoon tea and the big one .... till the calls of the flesh are saturated without fear of criticism.

Saint Atheroma looks on approvingly, her cheeks flushed in anticipation.

To finish, rum, brandy, Cointreau and lemon in another exotic cocktail called 'Between the Sheets', recommended by the aged wine waiter.

After the meal they walked along the bank of the river Dargle, hand in hand, towards the flat she shared with a group of friends.

"You seem to be very close to Wilfred?" David tried to make his voice sound casual.

Deirdre let go of his hand. "I am close. He has ideas in his head and a sense of adventure that would make all your Marrakesh travellers seem like stick-in-the-muds. It is him that makes it possible for me to stay in this place and yet feel I'm roaming the world." Then seeing David's expression she put her arms around him. "Don't go confusing what I've just told you with other things."

"Are we another thing then?" He demanded. They were holding on to each other at the very edge of the river bank.

There had always been running water wherever he'd lived. The canal at Lower Kimmage Road where he'd watched pieces of wood he had gathered, racing each other in the current. He'd have bets with himself as to which one would win. No bookies to take the spoils in those days. Then the Dodder, a proper river flowing upmarket from Terenure to Dartry and past the Dropping Well where he and his father had their last drink before he'd come south.

She pushed him gently away again as she asked. "Do you believe we can transcend our everyday consciousness if something important inspires us? Why should such adventures be confined to monks or mystics who hide themselves away from life?" Then before he could reply she had turned away. "It's time I was off."

"I don't know." David followed her. "Maybe I'm another victim of neutrality. I've dreamed of being a front line trooper, doing heroic deeds, but I'm not sure if I would just turn out to be yet another coward when the chips were down." Catching Deirdre by the arm he pulled her towards him. "I want to be able to meet your expectations, you know that, don't you?"

"Don't be a baby." She drew back. "I'm confused enough in myself so I can hardly expect you to suddenly come up with a miraculous response to questions that I suspect don't have a set solution." She sounded harsh. "And don't go personalizing every challenge that happens to cross your path." Staring into the river Deirdre sighed. "Sometimes the only way is to follow your instinct blindly till you find an answer. Even if you don't discover what you were seeking the journey itself can lift you out of the mire."

He turned her head towards him so that her lips were close to his but she shook him off.

"Drop me off home now and next time we meet I'm going to show you some of the places where I was dragged up and maybe if I'm in the mood I'll treat you to one or two other things that might just interest you." She laughed at his serious expression. "Are you on or not?"

They walked back along the river path in silence.

"I'm on alright," he replied stopping at the gate. "And don't go mistaking me for one of those porters that lugs other people's baggage up the Himalayas. I've got my own agenda on this journey."

"Come here." She gripped his shoulders tightly and pulled him roughly towards her. Behind her he could see the curtains of an upstairs room being pulled closed.

The Eagle has landed ... and the surface of the moon was fine and powdery.

"I'll leave the drink out for now, David, if you don't mind. It's real courage I need at this moment." Fintan's eyes fixed on the psychiatrist as he settled himself into one of the fireside chairs at the doctor's house, late one May afternoon. "I suppose there isn't much you have not been privy to even in your short life, what with the work you do. I can tell you have the gift of listening, so I'd better just get on with it."

When he'd arrived David had ushered him into his sitting room. Now, as the doctor reclined in the chair opposite the priest, he prepared himself for a role he was as yet unsure he wanted. His new friend seemed to have grown smaller than he had appeared on that auspicious first visit, or for that matter when they had ventured out on the town together.

"Take your time, Fintan, and don't fret yourself about appearances. The reason I'm here at all is because I recognised at an early age that outward image has little bearing on inner reality." David looked away from his friend and sat further back into his chair, waiting. *Keats, another in the TB clan, had shown him that the path is open to those who are capable of uncertainties, mysteries, doubts, without any irritable reaching after fact.*

"You have a way of saying things." The priest smiled, some of his old bluster returning. "Still it's a difficult story to tell and, much as I need to confide in you, it's hard for me because I fear, in spite of how you respond, that I will lose your respect."

Turning his gaze fractionally away to deflect eye contact he continued. "As I've already told you, I'd learned to keep it all a dark secret until I came to this place and met the Chief."

A moment of further contemplation, then with a shrug of his shoulders he plunged into his tale.

"My mother's one dream was to turn me into a priest. But it wasn't just any old priest that she had in mind. An exact replica of her brother, Tom, was what I had to be. He, God help us, was the hero of her Ranalagh posh family. Off her and I would go to visit him every year, without fail."

He was talking now in a tone of one reciting an oft told sermon. *Monotony with determination.*

"Lourdes without the miracles; not that you'd ever convince her of that. Husband and other offspring forgotten, as if they never existed. Mind you, Doctor," his lip curled in a kind of self disdain, "I have to admit to you that the special treatment made me feel rather important at first."

Fintan drew a packet of cigarettes from his jacket pocket and lit one. "I'm not much of a smoker, but a drag or two from this will help me now." Pausing while he blew the smoke towards the ceiling he watched it drift away. "My short flirtation with egotism came to an abrupt ending, I can tell you. Tom would take us in his car, he called it 'the motor', to Bray. We'd stop at a pub, always the same one in Shankill. I'd sit outside with my packet of Rolos wondering how long it would be before they returned all giggly and full of hot air.

"Bye the way, I used to count the number of cars that drove past me while I waited. I'm quite an expert on the different makes. A bit of a useless pastime, wouldn't you say? Not that different perhaps from their narrow world of self absorption." He took another drag of his cigarette using the smoke as a screen to glance at the psychiatrist. David's face remain impassive. *Fintan's a wily old fox. I bet he has a few tricks up his sleeve for puffing himself up again.*

The priest waved the smoke away before continuing.

"At other times the three of us would catch the train from Harcourt Street Station. I'd love that; sitting there thinking I was Mr. Sherlock Holmes on his way to solve a case. The telltale stain on my uncle's trouser leg, the clue that nobody else had noticed. Was he the evil Moriarty in disguise?"

David heard the priest chuckle.

"The Eagles Nest first, at the top of Bray Head, then down the prom to the Sunshine Cafe with the half crown that the blackguard always gave me, for an ice-cream. Knickerbocker Glory. Every small child's dream. Slot machines that paid out if you gave them a discreet thump on the side." His grin broadened at the memory. "Then straight on to the bumping cars, wonderful, if it wasn't for the uncle sitting there beside me. And, of course, what charmed my mother but embarrassed the life out of me, was everyone going, yes Father this, and yes Father that, until I almost shouted out at their stupidity." Fintan, suddenly sour faced, fidgeted in his chair, his features reddening, the veins in his thick neck standing out above the stiff collar. "Still, when I got home the brothers were all ears. If I'd been to Kathmandu they could not have been more impressed."

Now the priest was smiling once more.

"Surprisingly I had a bit of the old pride left, it seems. I'd run along the promenade to the entertainment on the bandstand. You're probably too young to remember it. Always topping the bill was Harry. *My name is Harry Brogan, I'm the governor of this show,* he would always sing." Fintan's voice deepened as he hummed his memories, "And he was too. Christ he was great, and that oh so pretty soprano, the Deanna Durbin of Bray. A great one for a song even if she was past her best. Then Harry again, just as though he was Joseph Locke himself".

"Good bye, good bye. I wish you all a last goo'od bye!" The priest sang softly smiling at the memory. The next moment his demeanour had changed. The child had left and now it was the man's voice that came through. It carried all the heaviness of his stolen innocence and his sense of loss. He gripped the arms of his chair tightly. "Now we are getting there. Truly," the priest intoned, "It was good-bye to all that, indeed it was too. My Grandparents died; first my granny, and then within a few months my granddad followed. Without their financial support our own family grew poorer. My mother never forgave my father for that. When it came to the time for our annual visit to Tom, there wasn't enough money for the two fares so I had to go on my own. You should have seen her face as she waved me off at the station."

The two men were startled by the sound of the telephone ringing. Fintan nodded his permission for David to answer it but the psychiatrist shook his head.

Would that be Deirdre trying to call off their date?

"Everything was different." The Priest, grateful, continued. "My uncle had taken charge of a small orphanage, would you believe it? Just six unfortunates in one part of the house, and a comfortable flat which Tom shared with his frail and saintly cousin, Fay. She attended more to his needs than to those of the children."

A last drag on the butt of his cigarette and it's flicked it into the fireplace. Fintan glanced nervously in the direction of the phone, hesitating before he went on. "You could see them planning ways to avoid their tormentor. Early morning prayers seemed to be a prelude for Cousin Fay to invoke the threat, not of the wrath of God, but a severe beating at the hand of his earthly representative."

David enquired, evenly. "Were you on the receiving end of any of these punishments?"

"A shrewd question. In a way that was part of the trouble. Those children saw me as their enemy at first. I was at a loss to know what I should do. I'd always disliked my uncle but I'd not been prepared for this. Because my mother was spending her last penny to send me to her beloved brother I had to keep quiet. I would make up stories to take home so that she would not become suspicious. Each time I visited, those children looked worse. Not only were they forbidden to have any physical contact with each other and therefore could not offer comfort when it was needed, but they were prohibited from keeping any personal possessions. Later, thank God, when they realised that I was not their enemy, they showed me little treasures they had defiantly hidden." Fintan reached into his pocket and produced a small stump of a pencil holding it up for David to see. "Anything, even this." He shrugged. "Coloured stones, bottle tops, it didn't matter what. Then, miracle of miracles, a discarded bead found abandoned, like themselves, in some remote corner. They told me how their dreams, kept alive under the bedclothes, were of being rescued by a lost parent who would take them to a beautiful house with a garden and a family all of their own."

The Priest turned to his listener. He seemed to be appealing for a response, the first time he had done so since he had begun talking. "I had no dream of escape, no magic carpet out of the cruelty that I witnessed. Just nightmares that haunted me when I got home, like shadowy vampires that pursued me wherever I hid. Then the beatings."

David held up his hands. "Don't you think you should leave things there for now. Next time you come..."

The priest, however, brushed the suggestion aside and continued without pausing.

"Fay would arrange the punishments like great ceremonial events. Her frail figure spared no energy in the management of these grotesque affairs. The instrument of torture was usually a paddle of wood with holes in it. When the blows were delivered it left little evidence of external injury, yet it produced the same painful effects as the cane or strap, which were only used when the monster, my uncle, was inflicting a spontaneous beating. With severe crimes, such as wetting the bed, Uncle Tom, the tyrant, made the children strip and stand naked in front of his friends." Getting to his feet Fintan Dunbar pushed back his chair and strode over to the window. Turning around to where David sat he shook his fist in the air. "I could see Tom's fat sweaty face as he delivered each blow, his eyes shining with malice. I watched with the other children. He, an ignorant pig, and she, his first officer, her eyes glinting with excitement, her pleasure not derived from the torture of the children, but from gratifying her cousin's whim." As though exhausted from recounting his nightmare he returned to his chair.

A few moments later, recharged by a surge of hatred, Fintan continued. "The hardest thing of all, David, is the effect these atrocities had on the witnesses." He spoke in a stern voice, punctuating each phrase to emphasise his meaning. "Evil gripped us as we watched. Pornographic theatre, its sadistic purpose igniting the drab existence of all those present, a corruption of innocence. My own reactions to what I witnessed has left me with a bitter sense of self loathing, which is, I know you can see, still with me."

David Benn could say nothing to comfort the man before him for he was now so totally absorbed in what he was relating, that the torturer might be in the very room they were sitting in. The priest's voice sunk to a whisper forcing David to lean forward to catch what was being said to him.

"Then when it was all over, the arm of my uncle would encircle my shoulder, as this monster tried to cajole me into an alliance with his malevolence. This was more painful to me than forty strokes of the cane." Fintan shrugged his shoulders awkwardly. " 'My boy', I can hear him still, 'My boy, remember God speaks in many ways. Duty can sometimes be a painful exercise.' Then he would nod to his cousin and in the same self righteous tone instruct the misguided woman to get the child he had flogged dressed, and to be sure he had his supper."

David was on his feet. He wanted to escape from the room if only to breath fresh air. He did not hurry as he went into the kitchen to find glasses. When he returned the priest was pacing restlessly around his sitting room. Fintan waited till the drinks were poured then reached out for his with a grateful smile. They remained standing like two boxers waiting outside the ring for the fight to begin.

"Every year my uncle came to visit us in the country. Fay stayed behind in Dublin to look after the orphans. In her own mind I think she imagined that her piety would be noticed by the angels, and that her reward would be forthcoming in the fullness of time." He raised his glass and lowered the contents in one gulp.

"Good Health, Doctor, it's what we all need." Bracing himself he took up his story once more as they both sat down.

"My mother bless her, would doll me up in my Sunday best, after she had adorned herself in the nearest she could get to what she imagined to be the current height of fashion from Arnotts."

David found himself thinking back to his night out with Deirdre. *How much did she know of Fintan's history? His own mother had wanted him to dress smart but he'd never managed it. One brown shoe and one black one.*

The priest's voice intruded.

"Her clothes looked bizarre enough to me, but nothing compared to how I felt in the gear she had dressed me in." He hadn't noticed the psychiatrist's lapse. "It was as though the clothes wore me, rather than the other way around. I felt like meat in the butcher's window being paraded in front of my uncle, just as they do in those beauty competitions for women, only it was a contest without a prize for me. She'd give me a kiss on the cheek and say 'Such a handsome lad, don't you agree, brother?' My uncle would gaze at me smiling, then pat my backside approvingly. I'd long to be out in the open fields with my everyday clothes and the few vestiges of manhood that I had won outside the clutches of my mothers dreams."

There are Jewish perverts, but their activities are kept hush hush. Plenty of hiding places in the shelter of a Ghetto. Everyone knowns that it is hard to get much sympathy for the kind of abuse that turns victims into perpetrators.

"He would always arrive with flowers in one hand, and a box of my mother's favourite chocolates, always Black Magic, in the other. She would simper and curtsy, taking the gifts with the sweet smile of someone used to the adulation of men. Then when she had placed the gifts on the hall table with further giggles of delight, Tom kissed her full on her lips, caressed her bottom and gazed lovingly into her eyes. It always seemed to me even when I was a small child that his hand lingered too long on my mother's body to be seen as an ordinary pat of affection. You can see the quandary I was caught up in."

"It's as if you had no father, Fintan. You've hardly mentioned him to me."

"Indeed I might have been better off without one. He never rose from his chair when the priest arrived, merely shifted his position slightly to indicate discomfort, smiling, a vacant smile, the hallmark of his detachment from his family. The tea was poured into the boneless china and the 'Grande performance' continued. Brother and sister flaunted themselves shamelessly before their captive audience. Uncle Tom gave an account of his numerous visits to cultural events. The opera at the Gaiety Theatre; a dinner with a visiting Prelate at the Gresham Hotel or attending the first Rose exhibition. They saw themselves as Royalty and therefore not in need of real accomplishments. How they waved from the balcony of self-deceit to a stony eyed group of peasants. *Ad benedictionem gloriamque omnium universam.* The audience, David, were not amused. Nor were they transported by admiration. Instead they were moved by excruciating embarrassment. Silently the room would empty leaving the pair in their well of self admiration."

"And your father; what of your relationship with him in these situations?"

"I tried to talk to him, to get him to understand what was happening to me, but he did not want to know. Perhaps as he stared into space, that long vacant stare, he glimpsed some vision of life that was his happiness, maybe a lost love, before he had made that good marriage into the elite of Ranalagh." Fintan paused. "A weak man, he lost no opportunity to kick the cat. Every stroke of his belt on my backside was his revenge against the wife he could never, out of his deep fear of her, oppose directly. You can imagine there were plenty of blows flying. So you can see how I suffered for my attachment to my mother, a tie I was no more able to break away from than he was himself."

"I'll tell you now, Doctor, what I've never dared breathe a word of to another living soul." The priest went to the window and looked out over the gardens. From the nearby ward, coming along the pathway was Nellie Collins, her bag of cleaning materials clutched as usual in one hand. Seeing Fintan at the Window she crossed herself and hurried past to her next job. He poured himself another whiskey before returning to his seat. David seemed no longer the focus of his tale.

"My mother informed me, shortly after her hero had arrived on one of his visits, that my treat for passing my intermediate exams was a trip to the cinema with my uncle. Even as I got into his motor I felt something terrible was in the air, his sweaty body all puffing away like a steam engine reminding me of the orphanage performances. I sat as far away from him as I could but I don't think he noticed. When we got to the Roxy he made a big show of buying me an ice-cream cornet. The strawberry flavour is still in my mouth." The priest swallowed.

"We sat there in the dark while the trailers were shown. I waited for the cinema to fill up but Roy Rogers could obviously not compete with the All Ireland football final that was on the very same day. Then I felt his hand on my leg searching for an opening in my trousers. I wanted to be sick and to scream out but I could not move. With this sense of paralysis came the same nauseating excitement I had felt as when I had stood watching my uncle beating the young waifs he was meant to be caring for. His hand had found its mark all right. Now I was the prey, flies undone, open, all defiance breached as his hand worked on, intent on its own course. A public wet dream running out of control."

The film on the screen was just a blur through my tears. I could hear the music and the gallop of horses as they moved in rhythm with my uncle's hand. Up and down in the saddle, Roy Rogers was in town. Clippetty, cloppetty, his white steed held its proud head high. Into a gallop with a final toss of its flowing mane."

The priest turned away from the psychiatrist before he continued. "I ran through the darkness, full of self disgust, as if it was me and not the grown man that was responsible for what had happened. I got to the cinema washroom, rushing into its shelter which offered a strange kind of haven, and did my best to restore an outward semblance of normality. I did not speak to my uncle on the way back. He hummed to himself, lowering the car window and admiring the view of the mountains on his right as he drove home. At the door, my mother greeted us with a proud smile. Brother and sister immediately resumed their *pas de deux*. It was clear to me then that there was no way anything could ever be said. The next day I found a half crown in my trouser pocket."

"Murphy, Quinn, Joyce, Kilmartin ..... Pruneovitchskee."
Bernard Benn would reply when anyone asked him what his
real name was. "Just doesn't rhyme, does it?" He'd say, adding
with a shake of his head, "Not good for business either."

In the nineteenth century Jews were forced to Teutonize
their names. In the twentieth, Hitler forbade them to do so.
David was never sure if his father had forgotten his Russian
name or didn't want anyone to know about it. There were hints
it was a name to be proud of but never a clue as to what it
was. The desire to integrate was paramount as soon as he had
established a foothold.

"There is no going back for us, so it's best leave the past
behind and, besides, Benn takes up less space."

At school, David had been relieved. Each morning's roll
call confirmed the prudence of his father's judgment. Benn?
... Here. Pruneovitchskee? Definitely not here. Things had to
move on. Only yesterday the Stones played, in great style as
always, for the fans who danced the July night away in Hyde
Park. Brian Jones barely cold in his grave. The show must go
on.

"It's ages since I've been out this way, David. Showing you
my world, places you've never seen before, helps me rediscover
dreams I thought I'd lost. Do you ever go back to your childhood
haunts?" Deirdre glanced sideways.

He was grinning broadly. "Everything was different then.
So straightforward, even perfect, except, maybe, for those
brothers of mine giving me a hard time."

"That's why some people try to live their lives in cosy little
backwaters. Head in the sand academics. Head in the sky

theologians. Derby and Joans. A breeding ground for bigots."
David waxed lyrical. "Take my word for it. The multitude of
aunties I've inherited helped me build up a resistance to the
seductions of happy families. Anti-bodies is the technical term.
You're well out of it." David glowered at the view.

She slowed the car down and leaned over, putting her hand
on his knee. "Ever thought that you'd got a slight attitude
problem, Doctor Benn? But don't worry! I'm beginning to
think that I could love you for it."

They had driven up the narrow coastal road twisting its
way towards the summit, a sheer drop on the passenger side.
Deirdre wound down her window and pointed. Green polish
still on her finger nails. "You can see the coral strand from up
here. There's a large house just over the hill where we often
used to stay for our holidays when I was a child." He had not
seen her look so excited before. "Here's a lay-bye so we can
park and walk along that pathway."

Jumping out of the car she strode eagerly towards the cliff
walk, grabbing David's hand when he'd caught up with her,
then raced up the hill, refusing to pause until they had reached
the top.

"Listen!" They stood looking down on the gray granular
pebbles as the sea sucked them back and forth. "We used to
think the tide was breathing in and out, or sometimes that it
was laughing at us when we played on the sand."

Inland the stillness of heath and lake lay on their left as they
walked along the cliffs. She drew him down beside her, the sea
now only just visible below them.

"It seems a world away from St.Elba's." Deirdre whispered
as David held her tightly.

They lay still for a long time. He wanted to resist his desire
to envelop her. The pain of believing she was out of reach
seemed preferable to fulfilment.

"Are you the one that is trying to hang on to your childhood,
now?" She laughed in his ear, reaching down to touch him.

"Is this why the Jews took so long to get to the Promised

Land?" he whispered back, stretched out beneath her. "Can you find me?"

"Lie still. I can hear boats landing down there on the shore. Pirates, no doubt."

When the rubber bag was in place she guided him into her.

"I've got you now." She moved on him in rhythm with the sounds and the smells that engulfed them, rubbing her face against his. "Long John Silver." Deirdre laughed, except it's the arm and not the leg that's banjaxed."

My Jerusalem. Keep your eyes open. Not like other times, fumbling semi-drunk, ejaculating to evacuate desire. Feel her body rowing into mine. All distance is gone, all differences melted away. She's got her dreams and I have mine. Jesus, Mary and Joseph. Holy God. It's the same vision.

"Hold on to me, for fuck sake!" David shifted slightly beneath Deirdre's weight, as she cushioned herself on his body.

"Can you still hear the sea, David?" Her head was beside his, her dark hair covered his face.

Still inside her. My seed invading the Irish. Better than Champagne and Guinness. Archbishop and Chief Rabbi in their Black Velvet robes? This was not like anything that has gone before. Then it could have been Westland Row station for all I knew, or cared!

The bag's moving. They're alive. All the possibilities: Irish Russians, O'Manskees, trapped, not yet dead in the bottom of their plastic crib.

"Are you crying, Deirdre?"

Gefilte fish children with Irish accents. Down the drain, loose on the wild turf. What can be conceived there? A million possibilities; black hair, eyes of pearl, bent nose, romantic brain, heart, lung, liver and guts, all unborn and unbaptized, about to be washed into the earth by the rainfalls to come.

"Are you dreaming, Deirdre?"

This was not a journey to the silver vaults, the underground safes where rich people stored their wealth to protect it; from what, I wonder? Where all life is reduced by possessions, and the need to

preserve them from abuse. Boxes of jewels for the Caliph of Baghdad:
paintings and art treasures too priceless to be allowed to see the light
of day. All visited furtively and only reached with knowledge of the
password (The Dillon, I like) and a silver key.

"Let me, David."

She took the bag (smuggled in from Boots, the chemist across the water) reverently, and scattered its contents on to the soil. Mazuzaless, they passed over the Red Sea. He helped her to her feet. It's cold now. *Could they rescue the spirit of their union and transport it from this sheltered place to the mainland? It'll take more than a change of wind.*

David brushed down his clothing as Deirdre turned and pointed to his face.

"You're a right eejit. Look at your expression." She moved closer towards him. "Aren't you the moony one. It's not a bloody funeral we've been to." She kissed him, then grabbed his arm. "Come with me, it's off to celebrate we're going, mineh boy."

I am but mad north-north west: when the wind is southerly I know a hawk from a handsaw.

(Hamlet)

David waited until it was almost dark. From his kitchen window he could see the other guests arriving at the Chief's house. The invitation. Handed to him at the end of one of the afternoon meetings, by Wilfred. Not a word by way of explanation. In his hand, the summons to an audition. Was this the key to his entrée into the magic inner circle? He looked out of the window again. Not a soul to be seen. All the guests seemed to have arrived. He'd wait just a little while longer. Masterly inactivity was an art that Irish medical professors had earnestly preached to its students. Before leaving he went to the fridge and poured himself a glass of milk: a liner for his gastric mucosa. The hospital's own produce, thick and creamy from tuberculin tested cows. A few minutes later he set out for the party. He strode quickly across the pathway but slowed down as he approached the house. On the short walk over he'd changed his mind once more.

Maybe the Chief had shown a great deal of interest and gone out of his way to be supportive, but perhaps he did the same for all new recruits. And Fintan? Entrusting him with his dreadful secrets could be nothing so different from the confidences psychiatrists were normally charged with by patients. No special meaning after all!

He arrived on the doorstep.

The fiddler stood at the back of the large crowded kitchen, instrument raised to his shoulder. At the nod of the Chief's head the bow scorched across its strings. Shrill sounds cut through the air, bringing all conversation to a stop. Familiar chords galvanized the audience into yelps of delight, then on to the floor for snatches of solo jigs and reels. As the music grew faster dancers sought partners to meet the challenge of the fiddler's skills. David stood flat-footed, breathless in the sudden deluge of sound and light that assailed him as he entered the kitchen.

"Jesus, Dooney, you have us beat." The audience clapped after each tune while the fiddler, his expression unchanged, bent forward slightly for his pint and lowered its contents down his throat in one suspended moment.

"Are you all right, Doc? Have a drop out of this bottle." The Chief poured a hefty measure of whiskey into a glass and handed it to his guest. "You'll have met most of those here often enough by now to feel comfortable, at least I hope so. There's more than one in this place that will vouch for you and will be pleased you came, that I do know."

The floor filled with couples as the fiddler was replaced by an accordionist and the music slowed to a more romantic pace.

Fintan Dunbar arrived arm in arm with Eileen Fahy. Staring in surprise they waved across to David. Instead of coming over, however, they immediately joined the others on the dance floor.

A handsome pair, without a doubt. Might be twins, yet they dance like lovers. No attempt to conceal their embrace. Is this what I am being invited to witness? It looks such an everyday occurrence that it's easy to forget the hint of insurrection in the way they hold each other so closely. Tranquillity defying self-consciousness. He swallowed a mouthful of whiskey.

"You and Sarah have a shuffle on the floor, why don't you." The Chief thrust the young doctor towards the nurse and propelled them both into the throng as the spinning wheel song began to weave its rhythm over the whole party. Bodies swayed in unison, clinging together in step with each other.

Mellow the moonlight to shine is beginning
close by the win-dow young Ei-leen is spinning.

Where is Deirdre? Does she belong here as well, or is this walls within walls? God! Sarah is drawing me closer to her. Can she read my thoughts and is she jealous of Deirdre, I wonder? Some chance. Perhaps there is nothing out there beyond this room, at least it feels that way just now. How easy it is in this atmosphere to blot out the world. Deep insulin coma. Purify, start again, replenish. Is that the Chief's plan? It's addictive for sure, but hard to define. Perhaps it's because they are all so in tune with each other they move like one body, never out of step. All clerical, medical and secular banners to be left at the door and no malignant consequences? Is that the score? And the band plays on. Music, the food of insurrection.

The priest and his partner had left the floor and entered an adjoining room. Just a flicker of candle light from inside as they opened the door. *Any chance, I wonder, of us being invited in there? David looked at Sarah and held her closer to him as they danced. She put her head on his shoulder as their bodies moved with the music. Talitha cumi! Damsel arise! The girl is not dead.*

The inner, inner sanctum. Are Jews allowed? What a party, it's electric in here and it's not just the music. I can feel your heat, Sarah; or is it mine? Press closer. I'm partial to the feel of breast; ever since my mother weaned me on to that Tubercular chazzerai.

Sarah turned her face towards his, kissing him briefly.

She can read my thoughts .... Hey, what's this now?

She led him off the floor, not to the adjoining room, but back towards their host. "Here he is, Wilfred, brought back safely, as instructed." This time she kissed David full on his lips, then smiling at both men, she left. The flavour of what might have been lingered on the young doctor's taste buds as she walked away. Liquorice, with a hint of tannin and honey.

Sweetening me up for something, I suspect.

"Another drop of the medicine, Doc? The Chief put his arm around David's shoulder as he topped up their glasses. They stood side by side watching the dancers. Fintan and Eileen had returned. He was singing.

> *Is it the laughing eye Eileen Aroon*
> *Is it the timid sigh, Eileen Aroon*

Is it the tender tune, soft as the string'd harp's moan
Or is it truth alone, Eileen Aroon

"Lyric tenor. The Count Himself would be jealous of that voice, Father." David heard Eileen murmur to her partner, back on the dance floor, as the priest sang his questions. The Chief nodded his head a few times to the music. "They're a lovely couple, wouldn't you say, Doc? If I were a priest now, instead of a nurse, I'd give them my blessing."

As David made his way home he caught sight of Sarah hurrying towards a waiting car.

They won't know about Deirdre and me, will they? So why do they treat me like I'm a monk, I wonder? Training me to dance to their tune. Then switching me off. And look at her now, a bit like Cinderella after the ball. Star of the silver screen, only when the projector is running. Why has nobody told me the plot? Yet I am allowed a sniff of something that's a little stronger than any of that whiskey I drank tonight.

Christus Medicator?

Will it soon be my chance to be the fiddler?

David fingered the bundle of pound notes he'd stuffed into his back pocket in anticipation of a hefty wager at the races that afternoon. He fidgeted, uncomfortable in the clothes he was wearing, sweating with indecision. Not warm enough for a T-shirt, too warm for a sweater, June might be bursting out all over but she wasn't quite sure what her long-term identity was to be. Beside him in the car, Deirdre smiled at his discomfort. Not unkindly. Her linen jacket, picked nonchalantly from a well-stocked wardrobe, thrown over her shoulders without a second thought.

In England power was linked to money, fame or may be even political influence. Having a word put in for you in the right place ensured things like getting into the proper school or a job with a well-known city firm. In Ireland being in the know refers to knowledge. Insider knowledge. From the horse's mouth.

"Are you sure this great tip is not something you dreamed up? Drinking with the priest seems to have gone to your head." Deirdre mocked. "It won't be long now till you start dressing up in a cassock."

"Who told you about that? As matter of fact I think I am being dressed up as a saviour and I'm not sure I fit the part."

I'm confused anyway! In this case Fintan's angel is a tipster who is in the know. The Priest knows the tipster. Does it follow that the angel is a tipster or is the priest an angel? But you could be right, Deirdre. Everything that happens outside the walls of Saint Elba's seems a little unreal to me .... Trouble is that I'm equally confused about what is happening inside. Where the other walls are built with invisible stone. A trick pack with the Chief dealing. He plays the cards so close to his chest it is hard to tell which hand is the dummy.

"Now, if I were to touch you? Lightly of course, just to make sure that you are actually here."

"Oh, I'm here right enough." She lifted his hand off her leg, kissing it before placing it back on the wheel.

"Keep both those hands for steering the vehicle, or we'll be into the trees before you know it."

"Maybe Eileen will find us a double bed in the infirmary. It's all in the lap of the Gods except for this little bet of ours that comes from His stable lad. Bantry Bay, the password to eternal riches. Not a magpie in sight. Close all the windows. Tra Li here we come."

Beyond Killarney they reached the rocky coastline of the Atlantic, slowing down near the shores of Lough Caragh at the foot of the Seefin mountains. A small road took them to the lakeside where they sat together looking into the heavily-stocked brown waters. Even the quick-witted trout were lulled into a false sense of security by the peace. Sitting ducks: soon they'd be fodder for the self-importance of opinionated tourists with fancy accents.

"As we're not that far from Killorgin and the old Puck Fair perhaps we could do a bit of horse-trading ourselves?" David leant across and kissed her, undoing the top button of her blouse, her jacket slipping back off her shoulders.

"What sort of a question is that, I'd like to know?"

"You've nothing to fear." David soothed. "My ancestors were men of the road and have travelled the same path as your own peddlers, though that's sometimes forgotten. It's just a bit of honest barter I'm after." David roughly undid the remaining buttons and pulled the blouse off Deirdre's shoulders.

She reached over and unbuttoning his shirt drew his arms out of the sleeves.

"An eye for an eye then. You've no cross around your neck."

"Shouldn't you have fringes around yours?"

He licked his fingers and drew them across her breasts till he felt her nipples harden under his hand. She put her head back. Closed eyes, then smiling out through slits. A honeyed

84

smile that basked in its own pleasure. Her own hand between her legs. Then pressing the wet tips of fingers to his lips. Morse Code made easy. "It seems ages since we made love."

How many centuries of scholarly works have gone into building the barriers between Jew and Gentile? Maybe their authors imagined themselves as saintly souls on some great purifying crusade. With what in mind I wonder?

"Christ, be careful, David."

Ours is the voice of humanity from the Garden of Eden; before the Church or the rabbinical exegesists got their claws into Eve. Great power-crazy puppeteers in the sky feathering their own nests. Maybe they couldn't foresee the Orange Parades dancing to their tune. Telescopes weren't invented then, I suppose.

"Fucking pervert." Deirdre lay back on the car seat, her head pressing against the glass window. Abruptly she turned to face him. "Is it hell and eternal damnation for the pair of us, or is it the Tralee races?"

No cobwebs here, just a lust for life. It's not garlic we need to drive the vampires away. Those Holy Biddies, with their heads in the clouds. Trading off their brief moment on earth, hoping for a better deal the next time around. It'll be love that'll make their yellow parchments turn to dust. Or just honest-to-God fucking.

The harder the better. Through the barricades of finely embroidered deceit. Johhny Ray forget your 'Ghost Riders in the Sky'. Now it's 'Lace-makers in the sky, Yippi I O, Yippi I Ye.'

"First, a cup of tea." David kissed her throat as she closed the top button of her blouse. The hotel lay at the far end of the lake, almost invisible from the road. They sat in its quiet gardens, waiting for their energy to revive before they set off towards Tralee racecourse.

David whispered behind his hand. "Those bookies look a mite too prosperous to me. More like traveling salesmen on their pulpits.

"Maybe they'll throw us a few free samples then. Sure to draw the crowds." Deirdre was heading to the bar. A Gliding swan. When she emerged carrying two pints of Guinness, he, like most of the other spectators, was still inspecting the prices being touted by the layers. Everyone followed the changes in odds that were being chalked up as bait for the mug punters who behaved as if their lives depended on getting the best deal on their selection. They'd been battered by hard fact for so long and survived to try again that they viewed themselves as warriors.

David waved his pint glass in the direction of the Grand Stand. "What's the color of the smoke from the tic-tac man, I wonder? Up there on his altar. A signalman to keep the bookies' party on track. A communicating genius, he's where its all at. Anywhere else and he'd be arrested for making lewd gestures.

ANOTHER SHOT 3-1
BANTRY BAY 8-1
BALAMINA BOY 10-1
BALLYHASSIN COUNT 5-1
ROSIE PROBERT 5-2
TRUSABRA 7-2

"You'll not beat Hannigan's prices."

"What would you know about it?" Deirdre's words were cut short.

Small men, red-haired men, black-haired men, no-haired men, miraculously powerful, pushed aside all obstacles, and hurtled like a herd of cattle towards certain death. Battling to part with their money, outstretched arms begged to be relieved of hard earned wages.

David flung himself into the fray, drawing strength from the sight of his horse's odds falling rapidly. Even Moses would have been satisfied with the speed and depth of belief in the message.

Sevens then sixes. Women and children last. Forgive me Father if I have sinned.

"Five score on Bantry." David's wad was flung contemptuously into the rapidly filling satchel as the real men laid in with wads as thick as their necks.

There goes the life's savings. Thank you, Lord, for the fives. Is that red smoke from the tic tac? This tip must be from heaven or is it hell? The odds are falling like the Wall Street crash.

"Let's get to a good position so that we don't miss the action, Deirdre, not that it is necessary to run this race. Cut and dried, please be to God." She leaned over to shout in his ear.

He threw his hands in the air. "How the fuck did you get sixes when I nearly sacrificed my life for lesser odds? No, don't tell me. Insider information, if ever I saw it."

They pushed through the crowd, weaving and dodging their way to the top of the stand as the race started.

"Can't see a frigging thing. I'm the dwarf here."

"Will you stop ranting and squeeze in there in front of me." Deirdre grabbed his arm and manoeuvred him into a tiny gap on the step below her.

"Would you credit that? It's Ballyhassin Count and nothing else. Break a leg will you. Do the decent thing and drop dead!" Through the wall of heads David caught a glimpse of the runners as they passed the stands for the first time.

I'm on my tippy toes reciting the Lord's prayer. Are YOU receiving me? Over. Now where's that super horse?

Still unable to get a view of the race he gave up the struggle and contented himself with trying to hear the race commentary on the loudspeaker system.

Minutes later the crowd began to cheer wildly.

"Are you wearing blinkers, David, that you can't see our fellow streaking past those pathetic mules, or are you still the doubting Thomas? Didn't you tell me the tip came from above?" Deirdre yelled.

"Good man, Garnie, an armchair ride I'd say. Not only the best horse but the best jockey as well." Confidence restored, David grabbed his lover's arm. He'd grown a few feet. "Never a doubt, really, he bloody strolled in. Let's get to the bookies before they're swamped." They battled their way back towards the dazed layers, satchels now open as wide as their mouths. Punters, in their hundreds, had taken the priest's tip as Gospel.

They lined up with hands outstretched, aching with the joys of such unexpected exercise.

Meeting again under the stand, David pointed to the bulge in his pocket. "Ever felt one as big as that, have you, duckie?"

"Only outstripped by the size of your head, my lad. Just be careful it doesn't fall out of your pocket." Deirdre steered him towards the exit. "We are leaving now. I can't bear to see them all give back their winnings. You drive. I'll sit and count the winnings. I suppose you know this countryside like the back of your hand, so I'll leave it to you."

David thumbed the worn five-pound notes, repeating the procedure a second time. "Some more tips like that from Fintan's pal and I'll become a Catholic. Then I could cross myself just like everyone else in this country when I see a funeral coming. People look at me when I don't, so maybe I could just do it and pretend I am Christian, you're thinking? But that's risky. You have to be careful when you're dealing with the Gods you know. They are on the *keevie*. Waiting for us mortals to slip up. When we add a *kina-hora it* is like a Yiddishy form of having a word in his ear. Hoping for protection from above. Asking your da to look after you."

"It sounds like an incurable disease rather than a cure. But I think I am getting used to this."

Laughing the lovers headed back towards Killarney.

"For you and I have a guardian angel on high, with nothing to do: but to give to you and to give to me ...... Kina-horas for ever more."

They drove through the town, leaving the jaunting cars with their camera-laden cargoes behind. Choosing the road to Kenmare, they travelled a few miles into the wooded hills. David pointed excitedly towards an opening in the tall pines lining the hillside. "Look at that," he shouted. "But how come you know about a hotel, hidden away from the world out here? Next you're going to tell me that you existed before you met me.

"The magical powers of Sidhe," she countered. "Wasn't I a tourist guide for the Lepra folk in the otherworld, so count your blessings for 'the knowledge'."

This is her true habitat. Light flickering through overhanging leaves, varying the shades of color in her skin. The Vietcong have proved they can harness nature's bounty to camouflage themselves from the invaders. As a bonus the native foliage acted as a search-light on the frightened Yanks, a long way from their homes and a target for a sniper's bullet.

In the fading light the young Doctor gazed at his lover, watching as it kindled her Spanish blood, transfusing her complexion. A witness to Deirdre's transformation. David leaned across looking out at the small hotel nestling behind neat hedgerow at the foot of the hills. "This is where I'm going to hide away with you. Can there be anywhere so perfect? It's downhill from here on!"

"Why is your knowledge always so pessimistic? Maybe you'd be better off without it." She reached out. "Take my hand and I'll get you through these gates and up into our little love nest.

In the spacious hotel room a large window gave the lovers a view of valley and lakes that were only little pools of water when they had looked down from the road above.

David glanced sideways to where Deirdre was carefully hanging her jacket in the wardrobe.

"I haven't told you about the 'do' we had at Will Behan's place but perhaps you've heard all about it already?"

She made no reply, remaining absorbed in her task.

"You know that the priest was there with Eileen Fahy. They danced like two love-birds and then vanished into a hidden nest. Will's inner sanctum. It seemed obvious what was going on there. The weird thing about that whole party though, was the strange electricity that was in the air. Hard to describe. Even the people were different. Charged up, fired with energy and sexy. Like a nightclub full of mesmerized dancers." Still getting no response. "I'd obviously been brought in as a kind of witness, for the Chief and myself just looked on as if we were the parents protecting our offspring while they played. Apart from the odd dance they organized for me just to show me what I was missing, no doubt!"

'Look, David, I really don't want to talk about the priest now." She had turned to confront him. Exasperated. "I just want it to be the two of us away from all that for a bit. You keep telling me how little time you have as a locum. Let's make the most of it while we can."

He looked at her in alarm.

"Please, my dear, trust me."

He moved towards her but she drew away from him. "Aren't priests like any other men? My big brother certainly had his share of male hormones and it didn't stop him taking the holy orders. It's time those calling the tune in Holy Rome paid attention to that simple fact." She blushed and stepped further back as though she was about to walk out. "He used to come to my room and make me wrestle with him. I had little doubt about what was going on in his mind for you could see his hard on from the other side of the road." David looked startled but she kept on, her voice strained. "Once I felt him come when he had me down on the bed. That was the last time he ever played those games with me. He could not look me in the eye for ages after that." She stepped back from David as he reached out to her, trapped against the big wooden bedstead.

"Christ, Deirdre, I didn't mean to upset you." He kissed her gently on her forehead as, relenting, she leant her head on his shoulder.

"But, as far as I'm concerned they can keep their divine grace if it's meant to be a reward for resisting a natural urge for another of God's creatures. Those young fellows are the poor innocent victims of a con trick, when all is said and done."

She put her arms around David pressing her body to him. "And I'm not half glad that you are not a priest."

Abruptly she released him. "Come on now, Professor Benn,

get rid of that frown. It looks as though you can't stop that mind of yours brooding away. Analysis, paralysis. How about a bit of action." She taunted him. "Are you losing your nerve or what?"

David produced his wad of notes from his back pocket and waved them in front of her. "I would not gamble on that, my beauty," he leered. "Easy come" ..... Before he could finish his sentence she had snatched the money from his hand.

'Well, you won't be needing this ugly materialistic garbage, will you? See you in the bar."

Sarah gathered up the case notes scattered about her desk and returned them to the ancient metal filing cabinet. In a thousand years, cloned scholars would examine its contents for their doctorate thesis. The cells of these patients would have been eliminated from the national gene pool. She wanted to have some time to herself before Declan Lynch returned from the Chief's office. His closeness to Wilfred irritated her. The way he behaved, like he was married to his boss. Two minds with but a single thought. She giggled. Declan did have a wife and two children who lived in the town but he rarely went home, choosing instead to spend a great deal of his spare time on the wards talking to colleagues.

She pushed her chair back, the mug of Bewley's Assam — she liked a strong brew — clasped firmly in one hand, and perched her feet on the edge of the desk. Skimming through the news pages of the *Irish Press* her eyes finally rested on the film reviews. On her days off she would often visit the Savoy Cinema in Dargle. Swanky seats you could sink back in with arms big enough for two sets of elbows. What's New Pussycat?, showing now, would be cut by the censors. Even the title wouldn't be spared. What's New? The film censors had the same difficulty as some of her patients when it came to distinguishing between fantasy and reality. Ursula Andress with Woody Allen. She'd prefer a tumble with the beefy Bond, herself. Sarah pulled the hem of her skirt down over her knees then turned back to examine the newspaper's picture of Woody Allen, A bit like David Benn.

Her parents blamed the Jews for killing Jesus, the lamb of God, who died to take away the sins of the world. They said that there were more Jews in Hollywood than in the whole of the Free State. When she had invited Cynthia home from school they made their disapproval very plain, but then the Goldsteins never asked her back to their home. Now they were adults her old school-friend still seemed to stick to her own little circle. Didn't approve of Goys. Sarah sighed. David Benn didn't look as though he'd ever be strong enough to kill anybody. The nurse pursed her lips. Funny how Deirdre Gillespie was involved with him when she did have the pick of the local Bonds. Maybe it's his vulnerability; some women like that. Not that she was jealous, mind. Finishing her tea, Sarah folded the paper carefully, trying to control the fine tremor in the finger tips of her unexpectedly sweaty hands. For a moment she allowed her skirt to slip back up her thighs. The patients had been restless all day, mumbling and shouting abuse.

Vini waved out from under the blanket, incessantly snatching at the empty air.

Mahatma Ghandi, eyes staring, pointed to his gaping mouth, all the time doing his usual act of jerking his finger and thumb in a beak-like motion as he pecked away at the air.

Old Clarke, usually a catatonic figure stuck in a time capsule by the window, emerged from his trance to shout. "Dirty fuckers the lot of them. Who do they think they're kidding?"

A manic depressive echoed in a loud voice: Kidding Bidding Riding Siding, then burst into peels of humourless laughter punctuated by sobs.

It was seven o'clock when Sarah opened the door of her office and glanced down the ward. She would wait for the night nurse to relieve her and go straight to Wilfred's place. Declan Lynch had not returned. She assumed he had gone to help the Chief prepare for the evening. Did she imagine it, or was the carpet of sleeping bodies moving across the floor towards her? A trick of the light. Squirming figures beneath the blankets; some hidden monster breathing poisonous gasses that would follow her out of the ward? Sights she had become so accustomed to by day now took on a new shape, threatening to engulf her. It had happened once before when she was preparing to visit the Chief. One of his special nights.

Afterwards, she'd confided in her staff group. Psychotics know more than is good for them. They had tried assiduously to understand her fears but it had not helped. Instead she wished that she had not exposed herself to them. Maybe they thought she was imagining it all: yet terrible things did happen. Just yesterday that Manson tribe had ritually slaughtered the lovely actress and her unborn baby. It was there in her paper.

The Nolans, Sarah's parents, had brought her up to believe that Christ honoured and sanctified madness. Members of Saint Vincent de Paul, they had encouraged her to be a psychiatric nurse.

"Oh my Saviour, you were pleased to be the scandal to the Jews, and a madness to the Gentiles; you were pleased to seem out of your senses."

They would recite to her, even when she was a small child. Always excerpts from the bible, chanted like mantras.

Coming into this world, Christ agreed to take upon himself all the signs of the human condition and the very stigmata of fallen nature; from poverty to death, he followed the long road of the Passions which was also the road of the passions, of wisdom forgotten, and of madness.

Leaving Saint Ethna's Sarah looked back over her shoulder at the heavy oaked door she had locked behind her. She had been reared to feel the power and even the wisdom that resided in madness. Fascinated by the antics of those who flaunted their delusions openly, she listened to her parents chanting their slogans, trying to tell the two apart.

From another corner of the asylum Sister Fahy made her way to the Chief's house. She was thinking of Fintan. Her love for the priest was known to only this small group of people and their close friends. They had recruited her to help them. At first she'd thought it was a trick; she was used to being teased about her romance. Then, out of the blue, Fintan himself had revealed the extent of his self-loathing to her. She became frightened that he might even take his own life if nothing was done to save him.

Her own brother was a Jesuit who had educated her to the real nature of her world, giving her a thirst for knowledge. She had jumped at the challenge. Her school teachers, who regularly wielded the black strap on their young charges, told her that madness was a warning of what would happen if animality took hold and swallowed up civilization. Her brother, on the other hand, showed her that inside its monstrous form, madness harboured a mysterious liberty. The difference intrigued her as much as the man who was setting foot on the moon. Some of her reservations about Wilfred's plan were assuaged by Father Joseph. He told them how the Greeks had used theatre to portray the tragic dramas met with in their everyday existence. "Imagine," he had encouraged them, "those ancient Greeks, huddled together in their ante room. Before this sheltered audience the actors played their parts. Compressed into vivid ritualised pictures, the painful conflicts drawn from the private anguish of their lives, were staged."

Her brother understood, as Jesuits do, that we are often punished far in excess of our guilt. He'd explained that the very excess of suffering we are heir to can also be the font to rediscovered dignity. The resurrection. Now she felt that she might be stepping out of her depth, but that fear also excited her. Woman in Ireland often had to take second best to the men when it came to higher education.

Much Madness is devinest Sense
To the discerning Eye
Much Sense - the starkest Madness
T'is the Majority
In this, as all prevail
Assent - and you are sane
Demur - you're straightaway dangerous
And handled with a Chain

Emily Dickinson

What's this for God's sake? The same room as the one in which the Chief held his party. A Bach Fugue, can't be mistaken for the Irish Washerwoman by any stretch of the imagination. Smoke from sticks of incense mingles with the candlelight that flickered through the door of the inner temple last time I was here. It is waving at me. A witch's finger beckoning? Should I be here at all?

There's the Chief. Relax. Just stand and watch, like he said. There'll be a whiskey waiting if needed. He knows what he is doing. Marshalling his troops for action on a battlefield. Not kosher but these Pagan warriors will not be tricked into submission by any newfangled hocus-pocus. Smells like witchcraft, but then the priest warned me that his enemy wears a cloak of sanctity like it was his true colours. Those two staff at the table look familiar from the admissions ward, with their case files ready and waiting for a new patient. Not quite the same as their usual selves though, I can see that much.

Sexy enough to make the hairs stand on end. Maybe it's drugs! More people arriving now. Fintan, and Sarah? Can't be certain of anything though except that it's in deadly earnest.

"This man thinks he is a priest." The nurse addressed the admissions officer. Reaching up she removed Fintan's clerical collar, her eyes fixed on the tall impassive figure. The officer sitting at the table jotted down some notes in the file. "We have to prepare you now, Father. Nurse will help you undress." He nodded his assent for the priest to be taken behind the screens at the far end of the room.

"Now these buttons, Father."

I can hear her breathing. It won't be him, that's for sure. He is in another world. Some kind of trance. Must be the treatment that Fintan mentioned. Treatment, or disease more likely. They are all under the influence, but it's not drugs. All of them possessed. But by what, I wonder? The priest is totally detached.

What the hell is going on, for fuck's sake?

David stared hard into the shadows.

Ecstasy pours out, judgment is suspended like the click of a switch.

Wilfred Behan led the doctor into the adjoining room and directed him to a chair in the corner from where David could observe everything that was happening. The room was lit by a single candle suspended in its holder placed high on the wall. Its flickering light battled with the darkness. The priest, in a long white cassock, entered the room accompanied by the nurse.

They stopped for a moment as though awaiting some instruction. He bent his head for her to remove his robe, then stood staring into the candlelight. Figures emerged from the shadows and drew him into the corner, where they laid his body face down across a bed, arms outstretched.

What now? A love feast between Christ and His household; the apostles and all believers? Human redemption, through the feast of the flesh, happening before my eyes?

Sarah moved beside the Jew putting her arm around his shoulder.

Is she warning me of what is to come? I still have that feel of her. Her taste on my lips. Who cares anyway? Her skin is melting me.

Hissing down, the whip cracked against its target. Skin

to skin. Eileen Fahy, recharged for stroke upon stroke, as she delivered purification to the penitent figure who lay stretched out before her. *Christ, she is majestic in her passion. She pulls the strings of her healing skills that never see the light of day in her sanatorium. What powers have transformed her that she too lends her hand to such madness? He cries out. In pain or in relief? Is this a mystical act of faith to purge him of the guilt his uncle instilled, or is it a blatant display of heresy that I have been cajoled into witnessing? Am I so desperate for acceptance that I can lend myself to this? Such cries!*

Eileen Fahy stepped back into the shadows of the room through the darts of candlelight; illuminated for a moment, then blotted from view. The body of the priest lay strewn across the bed. Sarah too had moved away from David's chair. He turned to look for her, then saw the figure of a young woman standing over the priest's body.

God save us, it can't be Deirdre. What more have I to bear witness to in this darkened hole? Again the Chief has moved towards me; what for? Am I, like Cravich, to be restrained in a padded fortress?

"He, Jesus came to me and clasped my soul in his arms and put my mouth to where his most sacred wounds were." Deirdre spoke quietly, reciting the words as though in prayer. Then she knelt reverently over the priest's body. Each wound that had been inflicted by the whip, she gently kissed. He moaned when she gently turned his body over. His eyes stared wildly upward towards the candlelight, as he lay beneath her in a trance of ecstasy and pain. "I am God's woman. Where is your soul, you tortured man, manacled to twisted superstition that masquerades as law? Let me take it in my mouth. I'll anoint you with this blessed liquid."

She has gone, swallowed into the shadows. Her part played, but is it heaven's part, I wonder? All so practised, like an ancient Chinese treatment that pierces one's nerve endings to release the poisons at some remote location. No explanations necessary when faith can heal. The cure and the disease gift wrapped in the same golden paper. How am I to sort out one from the other?

Two nurses lifted the priest and bathed his body. Then raising him gently, they slipped his long robe over his head and supporting his weight on either side, guided him out of the room.

They have left me sitting here in the dark. Even the candles have been extinguished. It's a relief.

Later, when David rose to leave, he found the Chief's house deserted.

Earl Gray and Mrs Mary Gillespie resumed their long and mutually gratifying relationship for the second time that morning.

"Excellent." Deirdre's mother pursed her lips and kissed out their message as she savoured yet another mouthful of His Lordship's renowned libation. "Excellent."

Not wishing to be disturbed, Mary Gillespie raised her copy of the English *Times* and enclosed herself in its substantial couture. Her parcels spread out on the small table in front of her discouraged any uninvited guest and gave further evidence, if it were still needed, of her discriminating prowess.

Dargle, while lacking a Bewley's cafe, had its own rendezvous for the Saturday morning promenade. Smells from newly-ground coffee beans masked those of once-fresh fish hauled to the wharf side depository. Only the cobblestones remained un-prettified.

"Is that you, Mary?" In spite of all her precautions the fortress had been breached.

Mrs Monica O'Riordan, spouse. Her formidable frame announced its presence by the dark shadow cast over the table. Her voice was further confirmation of the theory that Force was indeed equal to Mass multiplied by Velocity squared. In another life Mrs O'Riordan had ruled an empire.

"A fine morning for shopping." Monica gazed at the trim figure seated before her, envy mollified ever so slightly by the few wrinkles she observed at the corners of Mrs Gillespie's mouth, Handsome enough, though, to be able to afford the transitory neglect of her morning make-up. "Sure you'd have no trouble finding fashionable clothes at all. There isn't a finer looking woman in the whole county. Your husband's a lucky man entirely." She hesitated before committing herself further. "Mind you, Dermot is a bit of a catch himself."

Monica remembered her one dance with the dashing Dermot Gillespie, who had scored the winning goal for his team and held the All Ireland trophy shoulder high for the crowds to admire. She had pressed her thighs close to her hero as they glided through a jazzy rendering of Phil the Flutter's Ball, and wondered, if the music hadn't stopped when it did, whether his cup might have overflowed.

Mrs Gillespie permitted herself a half smile. "You're looking in good health yourself, Monica." She gave the long sigh of a woman conscious of her public duty but unable to carry the burden without a modicum of protest. "Do give our regards to Thomas."

Mrs O'Riordan had obtained two honours in her Intermediate Examinations at Saint Martha's School for girls. "Well, I must be off now; shopping for my lot doesn't leave me much time to sit around gossiping. Good day to you, Mary!" Her mind fixed on the evening meal she had planned as a birthday treat for her husband, she bulldozed her way out on to the street and headed towards MacGirk's.

Mrs Gillespie gathered her parcels together into a tidy pile before resuming her perusal of the social columns of *The Times*. Harold Wilson given an audience by the Beatles. After a few moments she lowered her newspaper and glanced briefly towards the cake trolley. Strawberry Carmen Miranda flans, laced with dark yellow cream, stared back at her. Sighing again, or was it a purr?, she poured herself another cup of her favourite tea. She had taken but a few delicate sips of the beverage when her daughter entered the cafe.

"This town's getting as bad as Dublin, mother. Not a parking place to be had on the quay." Deirdre leaned over her to give a brief kiss on the forehead. "What's wrong with that tea? You look as if you have just swallowed champagne left over from the night before?"

"And you, child, look like death warmed up. What have you been doing in that dreadful place. It really is too much. High time you changed your job." Mrs Gillespie was conscious of her duty. She had a particular dislike of the hippies. And at this moment, as she gazed in disapproval at her daughter's hair, tied tightly back from her face, that was the word that she could not bring herself to utter.

"Come on, mother, we've been through this till the cows come home." She pulled the chair back, scraping its legs on the parquet tiles as she did so. "How is Tom getting on with his exams? He should soon have them over and done with, before it's out into the big world without his Mammy to look after him." Butter would not melt in her mouth. She smiled in a friendly way at her mother.

"It's not him I have to worry about." Mary was trying equally to avoid another brush with her daughter's wild ideas. "He'll be in with your Daddy's firm just as soon as he has had his little trip to South America with Dermot." She could not keep the note of pride out of her voice although she tried to sound casual. "No indeed, and he's going steady with Grainne Fitzgerald." There was no disguising her delight. She wiped an eyebrow back into place with an elegant finger. "You could do a lot worse than that brother of Grainne yourself." Mrs Gillespie looked relieved that she had had her say. Beckoned to the waitress, with a slight nod. "Would you bring a few of those shortbread biscuits, Geraldine, there's a good girl." She drew her head back raising her chin slightly. Good intentions now abandoned, she turned back to confront her daughter. "What am I going to do with you. Just look at your hair, girl. When did it last see a hairdressers? Go on then, laugh your head off. You'll come crying to me one day with your youth wasted and your good looks gone. That establishment you work in is no place for a young woman."

She burst into full sail. "If you have to pursue these wild ideas I'd rather you wander off like the others of your own kind to the Maharishi or Marakesh or wherever." She was breathing hard, her delicate nostrils puffed out into tiny perfect shaped globes. She had cottoned on to the fact that some people of standing seemed to attach a certain Kudos if they caught a plane rather than a bus. "God knows what goes on in that nut-house. Isn't that madman Reilly in charge of it?" A triumphant smile before she returned to her tight lipped stance. "Need I continue?"

"There is more sanity behind the walls of Saint Elba's than in many of the ever-so-grand houses, like the one where I was brought up."

"You are not calling your own mother mad, are you? Some day it'll sink in to that obstinate head of yours, and you'll understand what I'm trying to say to you, dear. Daddy and I were talking about it only last night." Mrs Gillespie lowered her voice respectfully. "He thinks the world has gone mad."

She faced her daughter square on, knowing the consequences of what she was about to say. "Your father is worried that you don't go out with suitable young men." She watched the blood rise up to her daughter's cheeks. It was too late to turn back now. "You know what we mean. There are plenty of fine lads that would give their eye teeth to be seen with you. And by the way, who was that fellow you were at the races with, Deirdre ?"

"Is that what you're on about?" Deirdre was on her feet. "Well, I'll tell you both, I'm not putting up with being spied on. How dare you treat me like a child! Just look at yourself a little, mother. Nothing better to do than shop for more clothes. Anyone would think you haven't a brain in your beautiful head. Stop being the model wife and start thinking for yourself, if it's not too late."

Mary Gillespie scooped up her parcels, and called for the bill. "This friend of yours, what do you know about him? A Dubliner, of sorts, I'm reliably informed although I've not heard of an Irishman with a name like Benn, I have to say." Now ready for take off, she pursed her lips in a sneer. "And if you think a mental hospital is the place to find happiness, my girl, it hardly says much for your own mental abilities." She planted a kiss on her daughter's cheek, then departed before Deirdre could reply.

The young woman sat down again at the table. Mother was not her priority. She tried to think about what she might say to her lover. All of them trusted Wilfred. He had lifted them outside their everyday lives. Adventure was not the sole preserve of flower people gathering on campus in Chicago or the shine at Knock. They had no need to explain their lives to her mother or her precious friends. Didn't love, like its brother, hate, cross all boundaries that might threaten to contradict its purpose? Love was a bird of Paradise, a transformation that sloughed off the pitiful inadequacies of reason. David would understand. The sounds of clinking china cups made her look up. Solemn voices debated the pros and cons of chocolate gateau and rich Dundee fruitcake. Business men in pin-striped suits, made to measure from the only bespoke tailor in town, ordered black coffee and plain digestive biscuits.

After waiting a while longer, to be sure she would not bump in to her mother again, she strolled out into the fresh air.

Blood from David's shaving wound dripped in large globules on to the front page of the *Irish Times*. The last grains of sand in the egg timer drained silently away, unnoticed. A picture of Bogside rioters, who had learnt their lessons from students in Paris, was just visible through the stains. Cohn-Bendit had shown them the way. Nothing on any of the other pages about a happening at Saint Elba's. The gash under his left nostril, where he'd nicked himself with the new razor blade, stung from an iodized stick he'd used to try and stem the bleeding. In spite of the pain, the news, though it came from outside the Free State, began to improve David's mood.

Father will be pleased. Neutrality was losing its grip. The enemy will be changing their shirts again. From brown to black to blue — they'll soon be running out of colours. Perhaps they'll choose orange next.

On the ward the anaesthetist was checking his gas cylinders. A half grunt in David's direction combined with a nod to Sister. Ready. Steady. Sarah and Eileen, one on either side of the bed, laid a gentle hand on their patient as the electricity shuddered through her flaccid muscles. Prometheus O'Shea slipped outside for a quick Gold Flake.

Not much connection between these woman and the fiery rebels getting their priest prepared for a shock treatment that was not in the standard textbooks of psychiatry. None of them seem to find last night's events even worth a mention. Just another way of obliterating painful experiences at the crack of a whip. Miracles might be coming back into fashion.

Sarah beckoned towards David as soon as the anaesthetist had left. "By the looks of you, Doctor, you are in need of some therapy yourself. Come into the office and we'll make you a cup of tea."

These people are a different race to the vibrating swashbucklers of yesterday. A cup of tea, Doctor, a piece of me Ma's cake? Not the utterances of gladiators battling to unlock the tortuous chains that bind their priest. That's for sure. Sir and Lady Galahad - After the Ball was Over.

David sat reading the racing column of the *Press* while the patients were wheeled back to their wards. Nap selection for the day was Fleeting Moment.

The odds-on forecast price was not inviting. He finished his tea and scooped up the last few crumbs of cake from his plate.

Give Deirdre a ring. She'll make it right ... if she loves me and is not just using me. Perhaps she is praying for guidance? Our Father - whose seed I've swallowed.

Are we all footmen of a made up boss who nobody has ever seen? After two thousand years why try and stop the merry-go-round?

He put down the newspaper and gingerly examined the scab of his early morning wound with a fingertip.

Too much sugar in that cup of tea. Still ... why worry? Hadn't Christ Himself sought absolution down this very road. Then so had Rasputin. No matter. Suffer more. Suffer better. But look where it got Him.

A trickle of blood appeared at the edge of the wound where he had disturbed the scab..

David smiled at Sarah as she entered the office. "Your mother's cake is great. It reminds me of my own mother's baking."

"I'll wrap you a piece, Doctor, and you can take it home with you. There are times when you need a mother's touch." As she handed him the cake the nurse leaned close to him.

I can smell last night off you. Why don't I take you home? If the music is playing, we can all join in. Here Comes the Sun. It's all right. Sun Sun Sun. Real hippy stuff - if you can find one this side of the water. We could leave Deirdre to her priest. On second thoughts she'll like to watch us at it. Her and me and you, but not with your mother's seedcake in your mouth.

In years gone by David and his father had sat huddled over their Bush radio in the small hours waiting for the fanfares to announce the gladiators. Direct from the United States. The big fight. Clutching their tea cups while mother smiled pityingly from the comfort of her warm bed. Universal integration, fists across the water. Powerhouses of fitness and dedication with millions of fans plumping for the champ and invincibility. Just a few relations including mother on the side of the no-hoper. Smash the weed. He hasn't even got a name.

Phoning home now, he heard his father ask. "Are you listening to the big fight tonight, son?"

"Just like the old days, Dad."

"It's hard to remember some of them. Could there really have been a fight between Cohen and Kelly? You sound a little punch drunk yourself, David, so take care and remember I'm looking forward to a visit from you soon. July already so maybe you'll be home for good in a few months' time." He paused. "Anyway, you can bring that girl friend of yours with you. See if she likes the life up here. We'll all take a trip to the Curragh. The Prendergasts have some promising two-year-olds in their yard, I hear."

"I'll be there sure enough to battle with the bookies. Did you know that one of them has a Ph.D. in mathematics? What chance have poor mugs like ourselves?" David sighed.

"Everything all right there, son?" The older Mr Benn turned, as he did in times of stress, to address his dead wife. "What's with the boy, Ann? Something is making my hair stand on end." He faced the chair that had been hers for years. "What do you mean, he should have opened a practice in this house and never have gone away. And the girl?" He waved an admonishing finger at the empty chair. "Don't be old fashioned, Ann. We're not living in a ghetto now."

Putting the receiver purposefully back in its place, David paced up and down the kitchen of his house.

How do I train for this one, for God's sake! The heat of Sarah's skin as she had stood close to him at the Chief's. Red skinned. Renewed energy surged through him. 'Whormones' at work.

He opened the kitchen door and stood outside. The night air was cool.

Christum Medicatorem. Was he the Jew, the medieval expression of Satan's agent? The Devil himself, Antichrist? The bringer of the Black Death seduced into a sinful underworld. The Saviour, carrying proudly the crown of thorns into His heavenly kingdom?

Or was this Flower Power doing its business?

The next morning the Chief paid one of his rare visits to the hospital farm. Leaning over the sty he observed the sow with her newly born piglets.

"There's one happy mother, Jim, without a doubt. How many is it?" Wilfred scanned the squirming creatures nuzzled against the belly of nipples. "Eleven at least, I'd say, myself."

"Not far out at all, Will." The farmer raised two hands, fingers spread out, then a V-sign.

"Fifteen and three lost. She's a fine sow with tits enough for this bunch of squealers."

The nurse stood watching while the tiny pink creatures clung desperately to the fountains of life, grunting from their efforts at survival. A contingent of patients, who worked regularly on the dawn shift at the farm, headed eagerly towards the nearby Nissen hut kitchen. Sausage and bacon smells waltzed arm in arm towards them through the open window, heralding the promised reward for their labours. This small oasis of plenty offered home comforts undreamed of by many of the eager workers. Soon they would be holding their large mugs of steaming brown tea and mopping up their egg and bacon fat gravy with thick slices of Kennedy's loaf. In the land where opportunity did not knock this was next to paradise.

"I've got your bottle over in the hut." Jim puffed hard on his Kapp and Peterson pipe to get it going.

"It's for the new Doctor, you said? He's been over to see the pig himself." The farmer beamed his pride.

The Chief raised his eyebrows. "Wasn't it the Chinese that had the good sense to worship the pig. The shame of it is that a lot of people copy its worst habits."

The poteen safely hidden in the boot of his car, the nurse drove off towards Kilthorn Abbey, the occasional residence of an English absentee landlord, parking in a wooded spot hidden from the road. Behind some overgrown thicket a neglected wrought-iron gate offered in-the-know locals an established way into the otherwise well-secured grounds. A narrow pathway down the bank led to the lakeside. Sea smells, drifting up the estuary, lightened the air made heavy by the density of the foliage. The Abbey a great sleeping sentinel, majestic behind walls that stretched their crumbling masonry protectively around neglected gardens. Bending down, the nurse drew in the net he'd attached to a pulley the day before. The salmon, scaled armour shimmering, made one last try to struggle free of the trap, then lay still. Half an hour later the salmon had found haven in the pantry of Father Joseph Franklin, former parish priest at Saint Elba's Mental Hospital. Soon its sides of pink flesh would be smoked on fine oak chips from the branches of the ancient tree that shaded the backyard of the modest dwelling. Fumes from the smouldering ash did not bother the neighbours. The hamlet of Anoig embraced but three dwellings, all occupied by retired clerics. When the current tenants took over they found that they had the place more or less to themselves, the houses having long been abandoned by their tenants, made more prosperous by council grants for new build.

Joseph had little trouble in persuading his neighbours to join him in a cooperative venture, all the rage at the time when self sufficiency was the new totem of purity — for a discriminating minority, at least. Now this small group eked a living from the substantial body of home-cured salmon. A noble fish, it had the obvious advantage to poachers; ease of availability from the rivers of absentee landlords. No guilt feelings were felt or expressed by the fishermen during the execution of the act. Wilfred had heard that the same hamlet was blessed with an added source of sustenance. Only a whisper of course; it was rumoured to exist in the form of a white liquid generated from a pot still which had been bequeathed to them by a cousin now emigrated to America. The same colour as Holy water. The Gardai much too busy to investigate the origin of wisps of white smoke. In matters of the spirit they knew that tangible evidence was hard to come by.

Meanwhile Father Franklin used his spare time to continue his extensive research into the lives of saints. Long before the icons of the sixties began to search for meaning beyond the crass materialism of an over-anxious generation Joseph had discovered his own laboratory. For years he had dwelt amidst the insane inhabitants of Dargle's mental hospital, sifting through their thoughts and utterances for the key; the true pathway to the meaning of life and its passions. An eclectic, he fished in many waters. From Bhudda to Sigmund Freud, his exploration more exciting to him than travellers' tales that might start out at some crowded airport. His reading, a meandering adventure through waters as challenging as the Riddles of Erskine Childers' pioneering seafaring adventures.

His own vows of celibacy heightened, rather than distorted, his sexual insights. Like the psychoanalysts he studied, his method was to explore the inner lives of others by endeavouring to understand each nuance of their personality and their history. He became skilled in the art of projecting himself into his subjects and identifying so closely with their inner selves that he could safely draw on information gleaned from the adventure. Some, he read, considered this approach to knowledge to be an unscientific one. This did not worry him unduly. In his mind there was no contradiction between source material achieved by this method and the so-called scientific approach used by university professors in seats of high learning. The Chinese had already debunked the ivory tower academics and sent their researchers to work for half the year in the paddy fields. At the end of his career Joseph told the Chief that the insane and the saintly sprung from the same fountain. In one, the inspiration carried them beyond the insights of their times, in the other it bred frustration and a sense of persecution or of melancholy.

The priest looked across at his protégé, Wilfred Behan. Before him, not the eager young man whom he'd first set eyes on more than twenty years ago, but a serene and confident adult. He moved towards him and clasped him in his arms.

"It's a treat to see you again, you look as composed as ever I had hoped for you." He stood back, remembering the long winter evenings in the asylum when they had talked together. Not armchair philosophers, but soldiers in the front line. Their models were not the Saints that had been sanitized by pacifists, but men and women, with real substance, who had surpassed themselves in their lives on earth. From these icons they forged a blueprint for action amongst the insane and their carers, the very arena where Christ Himself had played his hand. They risked breathing in.

Joseph now sat and listened attentively to the nurse's account of David's arrival at the asylum and Wilfred's decision to involve him in Fintan Dunbar's emotional problems. It was he who had researched the mysteries of the medieval practice of the flagellants. Salvation through suffering? Redemption through pain? A Judea-Christian ideal. Their patient, whose anguish would help him feel at one with the sufferings of his uncle's victims, might, in this way, do more than just assuage his guilt. Was re-enacting the tragedy itself, the medicine? He, too, who knowing the pitfalls of such methods, had supported the Chiefs decision to enlist the young doctor. He would take them beyond such crude equations and engage the Priest's own consciousness in the endeavour. Such were the methods of Freud and his followers, he'd explained to his protégé.

The old man was smiling. "An Irish Jew. Quite a surprise. Not many of those about, and the few there are don't often venture too far from their ghetto. But whose to blame them?" He was quiet for a while then went into the cottage and came out with two glasses of spirit and a copy of the old testament. "Le chaim." They tipped glasses. "To the healer! He'll know, somewhere in his mind, the path his illustrious ancestor has trodden." The old priest put his bible down beside the poteen bottle on the rusting iron table.

The Chief nodded. "But this one's the outsider who seeks to be taken in and not the insider who is trying to get out."

"And the girl?" Joseph enquired.

"Deirdre Gillespie, like all of us, has her own agenda. Unlike most young women of her age, however, she has a sense of purpose in her make-up that matches her beauty, a beauty that many would envy. Her family are bewildered by her. One thing is certain, the doctor is besotted. Yet he is so unsure of himself. A locum has a very short tenure and that is not helping him to feel secure."

The priest frowned. "Yet they seem drawn to each other."

Wilfred shook his head vigorously. "Without a doubt."

For a while the two men sat in silence before the priest spoke. "He has come to discover if he can find a lost world. One that he can share with us. That makes him one of our own."

"But he does not feel that he is one of us." The nurse demurred.

Joseph raised his hand to stay his friend's objections. "Reach back into the very roots of time, and you see that it is Christ himself who was the Chosen one: the Jew who sought to inspire the world afresh. By his own sacrifice, he hoped, like the suffering servant, to atone for the transgressions of others. The brotherhood He preached has long been buried. You must take great care of this young man who may, unknowingly, be drawn to follow the footsteps of the Great Redeemer. The task you have set him may indeed help free our priest. He will show him the twisted pathways his guilty soul has followed, but because David Benn has come with his own agenda he could be tempted to travel further. He may be lured by powerful forces to travel far beyond his stated goals, on a path that we have seen has but a thin divide from mania, of that I am sure." The priest sat back suddenly drained by the intensity of their discussion.

Wilfred sighed, aware that his tutor was now an old man. He laid a comforting hand on his mentor. "When I listen to you I feel that I am venturing far from the bounds of my own understanding. The faith of those that follow me carries me forward yet I'm not sure where I take them."

"Focus your mind on the challenge. You are not some hippy person wandering the globe trying to cool out, imagining that a new place or for that matter a new thought will in itself change everything. Miracles are out-dated. Strife is the active principal of life by which the world continues. It catapults the mind into action. We are in the thick of battle, prepared for the what might be released. Our vulnerability must be treasure as it opens us up to new sources of treasured. The challenge lies on your own doorstep." Joseph's brow furrowed. "You, my friend, are a warrior going into battle to save a soul. This young Jew can help you, for he brings his ancient history, united with Freud's new skills in matters of the hidden mind, and this will be a long journey through hilly terrain. The priest paused. "But tell me more of his romance with Deirdre. So often love removes the drive and weakens the resolve. It makes their coupling an end in itself." He sat upright, smiling again, "And in my experience often leads the lovers to seduce each other into an agnostic comfort."

Will looked at Joseph, relieved that his humour was restored. "It might be so. Two love birds who elope." He shook his head. "But I doubt it in this case, for what attracts them to each other is the challenge to engage beyond themselves and their small ghettos."

The priest and the nurse spent more than an hour in the garden talking intently. Then they went into the house together. In the kitchen Joseph prepared some tea for his friend. He pointed towards his sitting room. "You see in my home a simple two rooms. Lining those walls you'll find the books that I cherish. Therein lies the word that contradicts the commonplace. The letter of Christ's message has been usurped by narrow minds that reduce the passion of his gospels to some mundane set of rules. The Church imprisons its followers playing on their fears with heavy chains of guilt and fear. Christ's house is walled in by such mediocrity, masquerading as goodness."

The old man fell silent again as they sipped their tea. Then he went to his gramophone and held a record sleeve aloft. The Bach fugue familiar to both of them.

"Listen to music and you will know the sound of God's voice. The accent here has a Goldberg intonation."

When the recording had ended Wilfred was smiling. Before he left he asked his friend a question. "How can we tell the Devil's voice from God's. Didn't Wagner dance to Hitler's tune?"

"One preaches hate and smiles with a sneer of self satisfaction then goose-steps in harmony with other causes, as though the tunes were the same. We must sharpen our ear to tell the difference. Each person has that task. Don't go to Church to hear those oft repeated messages. Instead bring something of yourself. A new text to replace the old ones and that will be the evidence of your engagement with these dilemmas.

That great and true Amphibian whose nature is disposed to Jove, not only like other creatures in divers elements, but in divided and distinguished worlds."

Sir Thomas Browne. *Religio Medici*

They floated through July, and through another Ireland he had not known. In small bars half drunken musicians serenaded Deirdre with jigs and reels that hadn't entered his Dublin fortress. He could only listen, while the others, familiar with the tunes, hummed along, tapping their feet in rhythm with an old friend. It would take him more than the few months he had left in the job to learn the steps.

Something for his children's children to think about, if they were living in Ireland. Still, he didn't suppose that Deirdre would be a natural tzadska dancer if he took her to a wedding in Grenville Hall Synagogue. It was a dance for those used to crouching down before they kicked out.

A few weeks later, Deirdre moved in with him to his house in the asylum grounds. "They're not going to like this. You might be flavour of the month with presents of salmon flying out of the sky and the poteen rising up from its grave in the dead of night, but me moving in here is going to set tongues wagging."

Deirdre held her poster up to the wall for David's opinion. "It's Cupid atop of a Purple Horse."

He pushed her empty suitcase under the bed with his foot then stood back to admire the picture. "And a little precarious he is too, balanced on the back of that old nag, though I'd say it's a good choice in the circumstances. Only what I'd expect from a woman of exquisite taste, of course."

Deirdre pressed the tacks in place to secure the poster then turned to examine her lover warily. "Even those with great taste can make errors of judgment, you known."

David glanced in the mirror. "If you are referring to any apparent blemish in my complexion the reason is simple. I'm famished." He pointed to the Andy Warhol. "Some of those cans of Campbell's Soup that he is famous for would go down well at the moment, so, whatever your friends think of you coming to live here, I'm taking you out for a slap-up dinner to celebrate your arrival."

"Out, is it?" She moved closer to him. "I can put a bit of colour in those cheeks of yours." Kissing his right hand she explored beneath his shirt, her fingers resting on the hole left by the old tubercular abscess under his arm. "Scars of war turn me on." She withdrew her hand. "Perhaps you can feel my own appetite making its voice felt. Just think of Andy's other little dish, those Chelsea Girls; that should tickle your taste buds. The dinner of yours will have to wait for a bit."

Lips pursed, hands on hips, Deirdre stood in front of a bemused David. "I fancy trying on my new wardrobe now we're into shared assets." A gesture with her outstretched finger to the trousers he wore. He stepped back in surprise.

"Come, come, don't you know it's hardly the done thing to keep a lady waiting'!' She slipped out of her skirt, hands on hips until he had passed her the cords he was wearing. Naked breasts pointed at him through the shirt, his own shirt; *had he handed it to her or was she a hypnotist?* She tightened the waist of his trousers with his belt and beckoned him towards the clothes she had discarded. "You can have your pick of that lot by my feet. I have my own ideas of what's on the menu for starters."

A half an hour later they left the house arm in arm. As David unlocked his car, Fintan's tall figure loomed out of the evening shadows. "You're off out, you two, are ye?"

Startled by his sudden appearance they looked at each other, hesitating, before they both nodded their agreement. "Hop in the back there. You're coming with us, and no arguments."

"Won't that make me a right old gooseberry?" The priest put his hands up in protest but nevertheless allowed himself to be bundled into the car without further objections. As they sped towards town he gave a chortle of delight. "It's a bit like being the best man at a wedding. News travels fast in this establishment, you know."

Quinn's bristled with the town's bankers and lawyers sitting astride T-bone steaks oozing with dark red blood. Friday night fever. The well- heeled workers of Dargle thronged together to celebrate the week's big deals.

Derrick, the head waiter, beckoned the priest to a table looking out over the river and half hidden from the other diners by the large foliage of a potted Fiddle leafed Fig bush.

"Seo Dochtuir Benn Derrick," As Fintan introduced David, Deirdre waved to Mr and Mrs Thomas O'Riordan, who had just arrived.

"Ta atlas or buadladh feat. An mbeud deoch agat?"

"What would they like to drink?"

David sat back in his chair.

Those ladies of the parish perched beside their men. Spouses picking daintily on their pearly pink schnitzels carefully sliced across the grain. Some of them look juicy enough to eat. Totems of male virility who called to each other across the tables while the men talk football or business in loud voices. Marriage made them feel they had got their scout's badge: they could return to latency with impunity.

"A couple of bottles of Chateau Lynch will get us started. Is that to your satisfaction, my friends?" The priest settled himself comfortably at the table, his back to the other diners. "You're glowing tonight, Deirdre. Sure I don't need to ask why, do I?" He gazed unsmiling at the young woman, who did smile back, as he called out to the waiter. "You see what the big fellow over by the door is eating? Well, I'll have the same."

"That'll be the Porterhouse, sir." He had trained himself in the art of restraint.

"Sounds more like a drinking place, or one of those Cambridge colleges to me, but he looked a happy man as I passed him on our way in, so I'll take my chances."

"Shush, Fintan, you're outside the walls here. We don't want you accused of excessive interest in things of the flesh or you'll be renounced as a heretic. Imagine them giving us the best table at Quinns after that." Deirdre looked sternly at the priest then turned to David. "Then we'd be dependent on this poor infidel to pull the medical ticket to get us a table."

"I'm afraid I'd not be the first priest to succumb to temptation." Fintan lowered his voice, gazing angrily back.

They returned home late, the priest having one glass of whiskey with them before wandering out into the night to find his own bed. David watched the lone figure disappearing from sight. He stood by the door rolling the strands of Old Holborn into a wafer thin cigarette and, lighting it, drew the fragrant tobacco smoke deep into his lungs, thinking about what the Priest had said to them.

"I am Deirdre." A long red shawl she had draped over her was illuminated by the glaring light in the hallway as David turned to close the front door behind him. In the darkened sitting room she stood in front of the flaming fire holding out her hand for him to kiss the silver ring she wore on her finger. Kneeling before her he stayed head bent as she spoke into the darkness as if reciting some ancient incantation.

"I will teach you the arts of love and war. Together we will open up the closed minds of the fearful. You who have wandered the earth know what freedom truly means. I will save you from the slavery of those who travel a narrow path. With my love I will give you the key to deliverance and release your soul from the torment of unrequited desire." She chanted the words, a priestess on her high altar as she cast off her cloak in one sweeping movement. Then with a great whoop of laughter they fell into each others' arms crushing their lips together. Their bodies absorbed into a single form, they did not see the fleeting shadowy figure that stopped to peer through their window before stepping back into the blackness of the night.

Cravich grabbed the door of his padded cell as soon as Declan Lynch turned the key in the lock. Before anyone could move, Cravich had pulled it wide open. He stood, arms akimbo, glaring at the frozen group of spectators. "Voss machstu mine kinder?" His voice, gentle, even soothing, nevertheless, mobilised the staff.

They withdrew a few paces in horror, awaiting the usual torrent of abuse. Instead the patient fell on the floor in front of them. "I can hear that wind howling outside. To me that is music. It tells me there is still a world out there." He established frantic eye contact with David.

"Release me from this prison, for Gods sake, or finish me off once and for all! What crime have I committed that you leave me to rot in hell? Tell me, won't you." The Jew's English was perfect.

"My body is poisoned. I need treatment, not this." He gestured towards the interior of the cell with a toss of his head. "You lock me away like a wild animal." He bared his teeth holding his hands up in front of him. "No fangs or claws. Why are you all frightened of me? Am I so different from the rest of you?"

Before David could respond, Sarah and Declan had darted forward in unison and slammed the padded door shut, bolting it behind them. The nurses turned to David accusingly. "Why was he asking you to rescue him?"

Declan, who had been assigned to help Cravich by the Chief, ruffled by his loss of control of the situation, muttered to Sarah. "He recognized one of his own, that's for sure." David said nothing, but continued with the group until they had completed the round. He waited to be offered his usual cup of tea and the newspaper, always open at the racing page, but the two nurses left the office without a word.

You see, my brother, they are frightened of us getting out of the cage. Quite right, too. We are sharpening our claws at last. The tanks are rolling. Not asking for forgiveness. Victims don't make nice people. Yom Kippur is for war. But remember, some of our best friends are Christians.

Later that afternoon, he hurried towards his house as he thought of Deirdre's promise to have dinner ready for him.

David pushed hard on the door, the wind howling as he tried to close it behind him. He called out. "The Banshees are out on the town tonight. I hope they realize that we are asylum dwellers behind these walls and take pity on us."

"Will you shut that door or the wind will have us upside down. Take your wet things off and come over here for a kiss." Deirdre hugged him to her. "I can see why this cosy domesticity is the great ambition for the languid masses." David nodded. "And it's great for the anniversary card industry. One for plastic, one for silver and one for golden when you're getting ready to collect yourself for the long good-bye, full of wisdom nobody wants to know."

He threw his coat over the chair and stood in front of the fire. "Thank God these houses are built to withstand this sort of weather. Like my reception on those wards today, it's plenty chilly out there." David went over to Deirdre and kissed her lightly on the cheek, then stood watching her prepare their meal. "Today, old Cravich surprised us all by his rationality. We know how to treat him when he's mad but what do we do if his complaints begin to make sense?" Through the window he caught a glimpse of Fintan racing across the hospital grounds holding a newspaper over his head. "At least it looks like we've converted our priest to the true faith. Look at him running about the place with his head covered. When I go to Dublin on my short leave, I'll bring him back a yarmulka and he can do the thing properly."

"I don't think that he'll be that keen now. From the looks of it the wind is changing direction," she called out from the kitchen.

When she came back to the sitting room Deirdre looked flustered. "So you are going home for a few days? I'm glad to hear it. Maybe the dust will settle by the time you're back and they'll have got used to the idea of me living here with you."

"I'm not sure, though, that it will settle so easily. It is great for them when I fit into their plans to rescue their priest but when they see the two of us together in this little love nest they don't like it." David glowered, waiting for her to contradict him. "Anyway, when I do go to see my father, you'll surely come with me. He can't wait to set eyes on you. We've already planned to take you to the Curragh and to show you off to all the friends." David cajoled. "He's looking forward to you coming to live in Dublin, so I won't have a reason to go away again. You'll see the sights of the old Jerusalem where we sprung from. Cambrassel Street and the Coombe. Isn't that incentive enough for you?"

Deirdre pulled the sitting room curtains closed. "You know quite well, David, that it's better for me to stay here. You only have a few days' leave on your locum time, and you'd be better spending them alone with your Dad." She walked back into the kitchen; returning with the cutlery, she laid it carefully on the table as David turned on her.

"I don't want to be separated from you. Why won't you come with me? We seem to have so little time. You realize there is no way that I'm going to get a permanent job here." He felt angry that she did not seem to share his sense of urgency. "Oh I'm all right for the stop gap, or the odd bit of dirty work, but the selection committee will be looking for the real thing, and you know it. They do the same thing over in England. Immigrants are fine for the lowly jobs, but wait till they look for promotion and some recognition, then it'll be send them back to where they came from." He moved towards the door, reaching for a coat.

"Your dinner is ready, stop behaving like a frightened rabbit." David turned back, picked up his chair and slammed it down beside the table, glaring at Deirdre as she put the sausage and mashed potato on his plate, "Not rabbit sausages are they?"

They ate their meal in silence.

"You're probably right." He scooped up the last of the potato from the plate with the edge of his knife and spread it on a piece of bread, adding bits of the left-over cabbage before demolishing the lot in a few bites. "It won't be that different in Dublin. No doubt they'll say you're beautiful, talented clever and enchanting ... but non-Kosher. A gentile shiksa." David recoiled at the odium of his own words. He went to the sideboard and searched inside for the whiskey bottle, pouring a stiff measure for each of them. "Let's quaff down this tonic and stroll out into the wilderness. After all, this is our estate. I always dreamed about what it would be like to have a house with land around it, and now at last I can walk through the grounds with my lady and imagine myself as the landlord. No rabble can trespass into this property. We are well-guarded by the high walls surrounding us." He laughed. "You won't find many that would want to break into a mental hospital, eh, my love?"

She leaned over and kissed him. David went over to the hall cupboard and drew out a pile of waterproof jackets and an assortment of old Wellington boots.

"There's gear enough in this cupboard for a fishing trip. I suppose the last doc left it behind for his permanent replacement."

"Do you think this lot is regulation hospital kit?" Deirdre lunged at him with her boots, David side-stepped the assault and grabbed her foot, drawing her towards him, her leg trapped under his arm. "I love you in buckskin." He stretched forward to plant a kiss on her lips.

As they passed Fintan's house, David took Deirdre's hand and quickened his pace until they approached the farm. The farm manager emerged from his hut, intently puffing on his Kapp and Peterson pipe. David called out. "All right if we have a chat with the old sow, Jim, we're in need of a bit of therapy?"

"Well, if she has a free appointment, I am sure she would be only too happy to oblige," smiled the man through the puffs of smoke. The pipe lit, he looked up at the couple. "Though I can't see what problems the like of yourselves would be having."

David hurried along the pathway that led from his house to the open ground. He was annoyed with himself for sleeping through the alarm, certain that he'd be late for the Superintendent's round. *Early to bed, early to rise, healthy, wealthy, good and wise. Father in a generous mood might mark him two out of ten. But his father had never slept with Deirdre.*

By the time he arrived at the morning parade Doctor Reilly was already busy inspecting his troops. A tall muscular figure, shoulders hunched, commanded the stage. The Killer demonstrated his pugilistic prowess at the rear of the procession with a double shuffle of his feet while he punched the air. A right hook followed by a body jab; he shadow boxed his way back to the wards. Doctor Reilly nodded briefly to his locum, then turned to the Chief.

"I'm off early to the races today, Wilfred. Carry on as usual, I'm sure Doctor Benn will deal with any problems." The superintendent glanced at his watch. "Now that he has arrived." He adjusted his red spotted pocket handkerchief then hurried off towards the main office, tut-tutting as he went.

The Chief walked along beside the young locum, while the two nurses in attendance fell in behind. "Don't bother yourself too much about that, David, we'll just get on with the few essential jobs and then you can be off." He looked over his shoulder to ascertain if they could be overheard before continuing. "There have been a few problems since word got out about Deirdre staying at your place. He scowled. "It's hard to fathom the minds of some, especially when you look at all the understanding for Fintan and his difficulties." He moved a little closer to the doctor and lowered his voice. "I'll be honest with you, it has me beat. When you think of the way we have all worked together to help the priest. I've even heard a whisper that he's a bit disapproving himself." He shook his head in disbelief. "Such audacity and imagination; hard to credit they are the same people now? I've talked about it to Eileen Fahy and she's as puzzled as I am."

They walked along in silence for a while before the David eventually responded. "Thanks for those words, Wilfred. I'm sure Eileen will not be taken over by malice, any more than you will. I mean it. But it's as though the very strengths we utilized to help ourselves now seems to be turning against us."

The Chief nodded vigorously. "Anyone would think we had done the job. They know as well as I do that our biggest test is still to come. We'll certainly want everyone pulling together if we are to achieve anything. I have read, though, that these sort of splits do occur when change is a threat to the old power regime."

They arrived at the administration building, and the junior nurses who were following had turned away towards the wards. Wilfred Behan led the doctor into his office. "To tell the truth, I feel like a General leading an army into battle, only to look around and discover my own forces are pointing their weapons at me. Prejudice is a terrible enemy. It comes in many disguises." He looked at David, his brow furrowed. "They know, as well as I do, that you have helped us understand why we need to move on from the rituals we've become caught up in. They are as frightened as I am. That is why we wanted so much to recruit your help."

The Chief opened the registers lying on his desk. "Sign these, Doctor, and just leave the other stuff for me today. I'll give you a call if you're needed." He embraced David briefly. "We're not done yet."

"That's for sure, Chief. We are playing with fire, and somehow we must keep the connection between our everyday rituals and these adventurous transformations in order to survive." As the door of his office closed, Wilfred Behan sat down at his desk and stared at the record books in front of him. After a few minutes he reached into the bottom drawer of his desk, removed the bottle from its brown paper bag, and poured himself a generous measure.

As David approached his home he noticed that Deirdre had left her car parked by the side of the house and walked to her office. He wondered how Nellie Collins would cope with the new arrangements, but shrugged off his discomfort. One of the secretaries passed him on her way to her office. He waved cheerily. The statues are on the move today. Maybe there *is* a miracle in the air.

"Get over here to me." Deirdre called to him from the kitchen, where she was preparing their evening meal. She kissed him. "Come and help me set the table." David began to lay the knives and forks out on the sitting room table as he reported the morning's events through the hatch connecting the two rooms.

When he had finished she came through to join him, announcing her opinion in a firm voice. "I believe that you've been a bit carried away by the ease of your acceptance. After all, you were a complete stranger when you arrived here. Now it's just back down to earth again. Does there have to be a deep and sinister meaning behind their actions?" She returned to the kitchen, shouting through to him as she then ran the cold water tap hard over the grains of rice. "Anyway, I'm afraid that lots of people make the sort of Jewman comments that you're always on the lookout for. Sarah and Declan are not any different. They've been brought up to think that way. "

He frowned, following her into the kitchen, watching her squeezing a few threads of Rathgar saffron into the water she had boiled for the rice. Uncorking the bottle of Rioja standing beside the stove, he sniffed deeply on the oaken bouquet of the wine then poured out two glasses. "Not bad this. Buttery, deep velvet, juicy and mellow, wouldn't you know. I can smell trouble at a thousand paces, that's why we we're given these superior noses."

She is right. It's all so homely here. Nothing to worry about ... if we never go out that is. She thinks I'm the mad one. What can I say?

"Cravich has got the message, but it's too late for him to do anything about it. When the dam bursts, though, you'll change your mind." He swallowed a mouthful of the wine then held the glass up to the light. "Come and have a taste of this before the Tsunami arrives. It'll make things seem better." He sighed. "In spite of it all, the two of us have come through some hard times, but here we are, alive and well, in our own little independent state. No one will understand why we will fight blindly to keep it though." He grinned at Deirdre, holding the tumbler at arm's length in front of him. "And we do have our allies to support us, thank God." Through the sitting room window David could see the boundary walls in the distance. "Still, better get the ark ready for a quick Exodus, just in case. I know this scenario from thousands of years of bitter experience. Never ignore the warning signs, it has happened too often before. That wall gives a false sense of security at times. Bigots have special powers for getting through even the smallest of openings. And remember, remember, the woodworm should not be invited aboard."

Deirdre laid the plate of cooked rice on the table, running a fork through it to separate the grains. Returning to the kitchen she emerged with a second dish, whipping off the lid for him to see. "Prawns, thick like yourself but nice and juicy and relaxed." She put his rice out and spooned the shellfish over it. "It may be traiffe, but there's love in that recipe, my little Yid. Just say the blessing for Dargle prawns and we'll tuck in. I'll pour the Passover wine for you. Lechayim."

Lying in bed later that night, David turned over onto his side to took at the sleeping figure beside him. He leaned across her slender body and gently manoeuvred her around towards him. As he reached forward to kiss her, Deirdre embraced him with both arms without waking. He tried to move away but felt her grip tightening around his shoulders. She muttered a few words that David could not decipher.

You might pretend it's all right, my Deirdre, but you know otherwise.

He pressed himself closer to her.

How little time there is to sanctify this wedding. I'm scared of what you'll think if you find out that I'm even not strong enough to have carried you over the threshold. Not like your pals at Corrigans, strapping big shloomps the lot of them. Give me a squeeze, Ophelia. Some call your being here with me a madness, but in these few moments we have discovered that their idea of madness is our idea of happiness. The facts of life they talk about, their idea of sanity, does not coincide with ours; thank God for that and a Plague on their houses.

The next day as he returned early from work he glanced through the sitting room window and caught sight of the priest standing beside Deirdre with his arm on her shoulder. When he entered they drew apart.

"I've asked for a spot of home leave." David grabbed at the newspaper. "It's not my solution, but tell me what you feel, why don't you?"

"Do you not think you're exaggerating all of this?" Fintan looked earnestly at the doctor. "Deirdre was telling me what you have been going through, and I have to say I think your reaction is all a bit over the top. Maybe a bit of a holiday is what's called for. Give people a chance to get used to the idea of you two living together. "

"I can see you're not out of that wood yet, Fintan. A nice rest and maybe a bit of sea air and it will all go away. Is that your solution?

I can hear your Cardinal talking through his tall hat. I'm surprised our radical priest is not waving a sheet of paper at me saying 'peace in our time'. He'll be advocating the electric shocks next."

He flung his newspaper to the floor. Deirdre glared at the two men. Picking up her briefcase she backed away from them.

"If I'm sacked from this job I'll be after your blood. Maybe it was a mistake my moving in here." Looking first to David, and then to the priest, she flounced out of the room before they could reply. A moment later she returned, flinging open the door and yelled at the startled pair. "On second thoughts, my dears, I'll steer clear of the stuff running through your veins."

Fintan shifted around coughing loudly as he drew the Gold Flake packet from his cassock. He lit the cigarette with a flourish. "She's a bit hot-headed, that one, moving in without a care for what they'll say. I suppose she must be right keen on you." He beckoned towards the door that had slammed in their faces for the second time then sighed. "Six months in a place doesn't give much time to deal with problems, and a smart lass like her would realise that she will meet the same kind of prejudices from your little lot if she follows you to Dublin." He nodded in agreement with himself. "Well, I'll be off now. Maybe I'll be seeing you two later." He blew the cigarette smoke out through his nose.

White smoke.

David stood up and walked with the priest to the door. "You're probably right about that holiday. It is time for a short trip home. I'm sorry if I sounded a little harsh with you."

The priest patted the psychiatrist gently on the back. "It's not worked out quite the way you expected. Perhaps, like myself, you're forgetting where we've been. It's easy to feel that what went on at Will's place, like the problems that plague my life, belongs in another world altogether. That is nature's strongest weapon and its worst enemy. People can rise to a challenge like they do in wartime, but as soon as it's back to the everyday life they relapse again into their old parochial ways." He shifted uncomfortably shaking his head from side to side. "We've tried to make light of what we have been through but I suppose it is only to be expected that the strain is now beginning to take its toll. The saints themselves would have a struggle to sustain such pressure."

Passing the Grand Hotel, David noticed that the green-uniformed doorman was already at his post. Taxis lined the road, hoping for a rich American, maybe a pop star escaping from pressures of fame, who would donate all his remaining loose currency when he was dropped off at the airport. The Americans had given generously after the war. Marshall Plan for European recovery. Bernard Benn still had the wire recording machine under the hall stairs, mint condition, never used. David glanced sideways at Deirdre. She had insisted on driving him to the station.

"You won't change your mind and come with me to Dublin, will you? I'll be lost without you."

"Out you get now or you'll miss the train, then you'll be grumbling about having to drive all the way." She pointed to a diminutive figure walking slowly towards the station. "There's Doctor O'Shea, the anaesthetist from the General. I'll bet he's off to the big city for a dose of high culture."

"Is culture a new form of medicine? Take each evening before retiring. I know I'm depressed but I'll take my chances without that fellow." He waited until his colleague was well out of sight before he abruptly got out of the car, proffering merely a glance back and a brief wave as he ran to the train.

Reassured that he would not be disturbed, he poured himself a coffee from his flask. The train, as though in homage to its steam-driven ancestors, gathered its latent energy like a shot put thrower, huffing and puffing, fidgeting and shuffling before it finally got into its stride. Whisked along, David sat back and closed his eyes.

It's easier to be a fatalist sitting in a train than driving a car. Lean back and let it happen. Father will be at the station. Dresses well but drives badly. Stops at the green lights and goes on the red.

Odd that the Dublin traffic didn't seem to notice. Driving tests were for foreigners. We'll pass Trinity College, through Cambrassil Street and he will show me the three roomed house in Lombard Street, his childhood home, where he shared a single suit with his two brothers. Done well for himself and his son the Doctor. The Coombe to Dartry in the twinkling of a life. Out to the cemetery high in the Dublin mountains, with a view of the Promised Land. Pity you have to die before you get to see it, except for Buddists who see it all the time.

Outside the scenery flashed by. Small unmanned stations were swept aside, without time to identify them; the implacable express hardly on nodding terms with their few planks of wood.

We'll kneel and kiss the ground above mother's grave, then joke about the vacant plot beside her that will receive his corpse. How would he prepare himself? Like the warrior, perhaps, who had practised rifle shooting lying on his belly in the garden, waiting for Hitler's troops to land in Terenure, down the road from the house with a Swastika shaped roof where the German lived. There'll be a welcome on the roof tops ...

Bally ... What's its name. Flicked out-of-the-way. At the buffet car the young doctor examined the choice of sandwiches.

Sodden or unsodden processed cheese. Discomfort food. David pushed the cheese sandwich to one side and washed down the offending taste with a swig of coffee from his flask.

He rummaged in his pocket for the Kit Kat, emergency rations he had learned to pack. Two weeks in the boy scouts had been sufficient to instruct him in the art of being prepared.

Wicklow. Slow down. Have some respect, even if you are an express train. Would you believe it. Smart people standing on the platform, some of them are wanting to get on. No wonder you stopped. Trains are the last bastions of the class system after all.

A large barrel shaped man lowered himself into the seat opposite. David looked with interest at the battered briefcase the new passenger was carrying.

Tinker, tailor, singer, farmer? Must be a tenor. My father will be playing the John MacCormac. "Down by the green bushes where she chanced to meet me." Then he'll tell me again that my uncle, who won a mention at the Feis Ceoil, could sing like the Count … if it hadn't been for the gambling … Listen, he could break a cut glass at twenty paces with his top C. All this nostalgia yet never a mention of the old country, Russia.

David looked down at his abandoned sandwiches.

There was a time when you could just fling things out of the carriage window with impunity. Before pollution was discovered. Careful though, that man just might be a solicitor.

MacCormac, MacCormac and MacCormac. Russia? All that is in the past. Why dwell on it? Always the same reply. Then why all the fuss about Barmitzvahs and Weddings? I could set this lot to music, the number of times I've heard the heart searchings. Too frightened to let go in case. The trouble is, son, he'll say, they don't really want us here, so it's best to play it safe. Chorus, all together now, watch the cut glass on the shelf … It's best to have a little each way to keep the options open. Time for a pee, but keep your eyes peeled for Doctor O'Shea. Why is it illegal to urinate when the train is in a station? Do they use the gases to drive the engine when times are hard? Soon we'll be getting fare reductions for passengers with large bladders.

Bernard Benn watched his son alighting. The spitting image, he thought. Put on a bit of weight.

Father looks younger. Lost a bit of weight.

Got a new car, Dad?"

"Why not, son? Now or never?"

Can we afford it? I'm the son and heir, remember.

"You've found this shorter route home." Mister Benn revved the engine of his Peugeot 404 and headed home via Kildare Street and Rathmines. "Less traffic this way."

David peered out of the window as they approached his old home. Everything seemed smaller. "We'll pop down to the Dropping Well for a pint before dinner."

Down by those arches and the high viaduct beyond. Dundrum, railway station and asylum.

Back home the fillet steaks were waiting for the pan. The potatoes all peeled and three-quarters cooked would be ready at the same time as the steaks became medium rare. When his mother was alive it had been a different kettle of fish. Then, they'd sit at the table, Irish linen clothed with candle sticks for Friday night. Lit without prayers.

"More than Reform Judaism," Bernard Benn joked, "more like informed. After all," he would say to his wife "talking to imaginary figures in the sky that can't be seen is a certifiable illness." She would shrug. In her life things happened. Who was to know why? One way or the other you got on with it. Survival was not a luxury item to be traded or reasoned with.

David watched his father put the chopped liver on two plates. No mazzo biscuits, like mother did, but a few slices of Kennedy's white loaf put out on a separate plate. Over dinner he talked about the hospital but did not mention the Chief's gatherings. Deirdre's photograph made father whistle. "Her genes and yours would make an interesting cocktail."

Enough to help any earthly progeny escape the next pogrom?

"I've something to tell you, son." Father shovelled some more chips on to his son's plate. "Your mother and I were like that." He held up two crossed fingers. "You know I liked to stop and have a pint and a small one after work." He shook his head up and down to encourage his son's response. "I'm not like most of our brethren who hurry straight home and never meet anyone outside their own little circle. I could say that those visits to the pub helped me graduate as an Irishman, or nearly."

"Sure, Dad, I know exactly what that means."

Bernard Benn rushed ahead. "Well, son, I used to meet people in the pub and chat about life and horses. The Irish love their racing and I've made a few friends of my own through sharing their interest. I would not ask them back, or they me, because we knew it was just what you might call a drinking friendship. Your mother would not have felt at home with them." He shrugged. "You'll know what that means as well. She'd been brought up in the bosom of a big family. Not frum, mind, but they still didn't mix with what were thought of as outsiders. I understood that; though she did like a little flutter on the nags, and so did her own mother, for that matter." He paused to observe the effects of his revelations on his offspring.

David glanced over to where his mother's chair was. Did he imagine it or had it been moved slightly away from its familiar spot?

"Are you telling me you have a lady friend, Father?"

Mister Benn was busy eating.

Each of my mother's dishes had its own individual secret ingredient that carried the smells of Ashkenazic and Sephardic cooks.

Yeats (assuming he wasn't anti-Semitic) would have had good sport with the names of those dishes. Hadn't they retained their own Yiddish flavour through the Inquisition? The Spanish Conversos for all their changes kept this heritage alive for their children to pass down, and they weren't exactly frum.

Potato Kugel. Tzimmus.

Hamman Tashen. Knaydlach.

Chremslach. Struddel.

Gefilte Fish. The Cookery Torah. Even those who eat traiffe can't resist the sweet and sour on the taste buds. If Proust, God rest his soul, were alive to try mothers gefilte fish, he'd soon forget the madeleine cakes.

Father's plate was clean. "Just a friend. It's been lonely, especially since you left. A man needs companionship." He stood up and started clearing away the dishes. "I loved your mother in a way that few will realise and I still have chats with her."

On their way to the Curragh the next day, David's father told him his oft-repeated Easter Rising story. While crossing the road opposite Trinity College, he was suddenly surrounded by soldiers. "Their guns pointed straight at my head. Suspected me of having a bomb in the shoe box I carried under my arm." He smiled. "I felt quite proud of myself, although when I got home Ann was dismissive of any heroism by proxy. 'It was only shoes you had in the box after all.' She sounded disappointed with me."

We crave for security yet long for excitement.
At Naas the race day traffic jammed the road.
Always money in Ireland for a flutter. Maybe horse racing is the cure for apathy. The best that some can hope for.
Bernard Benn showed his yearly member's badge at the turnstiles. Inside the enclosure they watched the horses parade. Kevin Prendergast waved to him as he led the favourite into the ring. Watching his father chatting to his many racing acquaintances David recognised, probably for the first time, that his father had a life.

Put your foot down driver. Four days away: more like four weeks.
David waved through the carriage window to his father.
Up, down. Down up. Which way am I heading? Never mind. Another four weeks and it will all be the same only in reverse. God help us. Always good bye, hello, good bye. I'm going Loco Apparentis.
As the train slipped out of the station he saw his father had turned to greet someone. Father's other baby. The apple of Bernard Benn's eye in the days when his son was growing up. Over the Half-Penny Bridge, a corridor to the Dublin's inner self. His work.
History to the left, history to the right. A clothing factory with a hundred workers, and all from nothing. Not much energy left for home or those Marshall's wire recorders and Buicks. Useful all the same: a bit of flash to show them he was not afraid. Not exactly icons of the nouveau riche. The man's work over, an after-dinner sleep while the family played cards. Self-made men can't cut their cloth to suit everybody. Not good at making alterations to their own lives. Even tailors. But beggars can't be choosers and persecution was a great motivator, for some. Berlin in the thirties was always flashing into the mind of Jews. Money is needed for a quick getaway.
Standing by the carriage door David caught sight of Deirdre hurrying along the platform. Dargle station, freshly glossed and draped with greenery, announced its readiness to receive

the tourist invasion. For a moment he drew back, frightened to reveal himself, afraid she might have changed her mind about him, yet impatient to see her. A group of young boys crowded together by the door pushing and shoving each other. Losing sight of her, he pushed forward. Then he saw her again looking anxiously along the row of carriages. Glaring at the youngsters as they jostled him he swore at them under his breath.

Bloody boys, they're all the same: ruined by their doting mothers hoping they will turn out better than the father. Looking at this lot of Yahoos, it seems unlikely they'll inspire even the cat. There she is. Her beauty is in her eyes, all whites with dark lashes.

As Deirdre appeared to catch sight of him (he was quite sure their eyes met) he was convinced that she hesitated before deciding to run forward to greet him.

How do I look? A bit weedy perhaps. Maybe I should have gone to Bray instead of the Curragh. Sea air restores the complexion.

David gave the young boy pushing to get ahead of him a nudge of his elbow.

"Careful with the childer or you'll be up for grievous bodily harm." Sidestepping the boys Deirdre put her arms around him and kissed him on his cheek.

Perhaps she thinks I'm someone else. Hardly two breathless lovers throwing themselves at each other, are we? Then I'm not exactly Gregory Peck. More an acquired taste, like Parmesan cheese. Bitterness is the next year's big flavour. So much for absence making the heart grow fonder.

"What's the matter? First you molest the young, then you go all distant on me. Is this what Dublin does to people? Come on, you ape, I'll take you to our favourite restaurant and feed you with hunks of blood-red meat to restore you."

"They don't have Jewish apes." David turned swiftly, his suitcase dropped, to grab her to him.

"I knew it was risky leaving you. Have you been at those *cruibins* again and forgotten that they are attached to pigs?"

Deirdre led him towards the parked car. "Try not to take the name of the pig in vain, if you don't mind."

They sat at their usual table at Quinns, sheltered from other diners by their leafy bodyguards. As the waiter uncorked the burgundy, David thought of his father sitting with his friend telling her about his son's visit. How long would his bedroom at home be kept just for him?

They drove recklessly up the hill to Saint Elba's, and through the iron gates until they passed the large oak tree. Deirdre pointed to it. "Our shrine." She crossed herself. "If it wasn't for that tree, I might never have spoken to you again."

He resisted copying her gesture. "It would have happened anyway. I'd have seen to that."

Noticing his brooding expression return, she patted his hand. "I can hear that mind of yours grinding its paranoid nourishment from every morsel I utter."

Outside the house they stood for a while and looked out over the city's night lights. "Maybe this is the second honeymoon." Bracing himself for the challenge, he picked her up in his arms and lifted her across the threshold.

I'm getting stronger now that father has cut the cord.

"Have you sent off the invitations?

Mary and Dermot Gillespie request the pleasure of your presents at the wedding of Deirdre and David, Number 4 Asylum Drive, St. Elba's Hospital. (Mrs Steinway catering)

"Do not leave out my aunt Beckie or there will be feribbles. We will have Mrs Steinway doing the catering for certain. Mind you, after her nine-course creations there won't be too much action on other fronts." He sat Deirdre gently down on the table then leering broadly he began to unbutton his shirt. "Let's see what you've got in that trousseau of yours." As he reached towards her she lay back, closing her eyes. He took a cushion from the chair and placed it gently under her head. Then, kissing her eyelids, slipped quietly into the kitchen and returned with a large jug of cream.

"Blessed be the fruits of the cow on earth as they are in heaven, amen." David poured the cream on to his hands and began to massage the liquid on to her face and neck. "In California the students are rioting to stop the war and change the world." The cream clung to her face, a white mask, and dribbled down the front of her dress. "They are fucking each other on the streets to embarrass the bigots. Such a small world, such a lot of pigs. In Dargle I am rubbing cream from the asylum dairy herd into the body of the woman I love, so that she won't forget me when she meets the permanent appointee. May he rot in Hell in the darkness of that sulphurous pit. Keep those eyes closed," he whispered to her as he turned away to the rummage in the bookcase, returning with a green backed textbook. "Diseases of locums." David read aloud from the book. "It says here that locums suffer anxiety, a nameless dread, a sense that the world is going to suddenly come to an end." He turned the page. "They envy those with long term security."

"Sounds everyday stuff for your average Yid." Deirdre slid sideways off the table. In a second she had picked up the jug and emptied the remaining contents over his body. The cream trickled slowly down his neck. She cooed. "Is this the way all psychiatrists make love or is it only the ones that are preoccupied with conflict at the breast? And don't disappear to the library to find the answer!" She took him in her arms. "Let's dance a bit, David! You can put your book away now. Just feel the quality."

He switched on the small portable radio and licked her as they swayed around the room. "I'm fixing a hole in the ceiling to stop the rain getting in." He sang the words.

"You wouldn't be trying to get off with me by any chance." Deirdre rubbed her wet cheeks against his face, her hands touching his body as they danced. David thought of his father's friend.

Would she have done the washing up before going home? Chance would be a fine thing.

"Up you come to the bridal chamber, my little cream sop." Deirdre took his hand and led him upstairs.

Moses entered the land of plenty. Broken tablets forgotten.

"There's silken sheets on the bed and a feather pillow."

He was doing cartwheels in his head.

On the top landing she paused. "Oh, and I'll be taking you to meet the Gillespies tomorrow."

The locals of Dargle referred to the inhabitants of their town as either 'uppers' or 'downers'. The Gillespies' residence, set well back from the elegant tree-lined road, could not be confused with newly built houses of similar design at the opposite end of town. Gable-ended to identify old money from *nouveau riche*, the garden, heavy with laurel and buddleia bushes, told the tale of long ancestry. Tall oaks looked down with tolerance on succeeding generations of residents buried with great ceremony and twitched their branches slightly if the wind was too strong.

As they approached, the sense of unease David had been feeling developed into acute alarm. He recognized the red brick as the material to which his father ascribed the great virtues of longevity and dependability: his heart sank even further.

No straw house a wolf could blow down, is this edifice; but what about the wolves that lived in the houses? If only Fintan had come with them, they would have been more secure. The priest had declined and Deirdre herself had not exactly been enamoured by the idea of needing a bodyguard to visit her family.

She hoped her parents would rise to the occasion, although there was little in her experience to give her confidence that they would make the effort.

"We are glad to see you, Deirdre, do bring your friend in." Dermot Gillespie beamed, while the handsome features of his wife Mary gave way to a genteel smile. David stared at her, fascinated by the likeness between mother and daughter.

Handsome no doubt, but her smiles, like hot and cold running water, vying with each other to find a suitable temperature, were disconcertingly tepid when turned in his direction. He hesitated before entering the spacious lounge that looked out to the gardens on either end of the house. Sporting trophies, and photographs of the various triumphant Gaelic football teams connected with the glittering prizes, lined the room.

You don't get this silverware for masturbation or running towards the bookies at the races to capture the best prices, that is for sure. What if they find out that I swim across the swimming pool rather than lengthwise? Time to give up smoking altogether, if I make it to the New Year, that is.

"Pleased to meet you, Tom." David returned the hearty handshake from the young man who had just joined them. "It must be nice to have all these brothers, Deirdre. My own parents gave up after seeing me."

She rolled her eyes to heaven.

The drinks arrived on a silver tray carried in by Bridie, the maid. Young country girls were glad of chance to leave the small farms, where they were little more than a skivvy for their families. David downed his whiskey in one gulp while Dermot served the rest of the company. He held out his glass for a refill as soon as the others had been seen to, hoping on the off chance that his first draught would not have been registered in the hullabaloo of hubris.

"So you're from Dublin are you, young man?" Mr Gillespie refilled the Waterford glass tumbler. Sipping his whiskey David sat back in his chair looking his antagonist in the eye.

Never had the words 'young man' been uttered with such distasteful innuendo. He could roll over on his back as dogs do by way of penance and as a plea for mercy. Alternatively he could kill this bigot, for bigot he smelt, with a Sten gun, as the Stern Gang or the IRA would no doubt choose.

Deirdre's brother, brightening at the chance to have a say, came to his rescue. "I hear down at Corrigans you're a racing man. Perhaps you've come across our cousin Terence Fitzwilliam, the trainer. No, ah well, but I expect you have read about his Derby prospect Inchnagoppal?"

"Indeed I have, Tom," David, now on his third, alias his second, whiskey replied, relieved to have the chance to restore some honor.

"*Is capail mear e sin.*"

There was a long silence.

He looked pleadingly at his lover to rescue him from the humiliation.

A right eejit I am, trying to ingratiate myself by speaking Gaelic. Delusions of compatibility. Like handing them the Sten gun to shoot me with. I wish I was a hundred miles away.

"We'll have a stroll in the garden, mother, before you serve lunch." Her voice shook slightly as she spoke. "Give us your hand, David."

She led him out through the French windows aware of the disapproving glances as she did so.

Outside, David withdrew his hand from hers and stretching his body, breathed in the fresh morning air.

"I'm sorry, darling." She tried to take his arm again but he drew away from her. They walked a short way down the path bisecting the neatly trimmed lawn. Reaching a garden seat that was sheltered from the gaze of those in the house, she drew him down beside her. When he looked across at her, he saw that she was crying.

"Don't worry, my dear," he put an arm around her. "I should be able to cope with this; after all I have plenty of experience. A few thousand years perhaps." He felt her flinch he leaned over and kissed her. "It brings out the worst in us all, I'm afraid."

"I just wanted you to see my bedroom, where I had my own dreams, but not like this." Deirdre whispered her voice mournful. "You're not the dream lover they planned for me. Another trophy on the mantelpiece for them to show off to the neighbours." She kissed him back. Managing to smile they returned to the house for lunch. "That's a great garden, Mr Gillespie. Do you look after it yourself or do you have a gardener to help?"

"I wish I had the time, dear boy. I wish I had the time. Up early, on the job all day and often get home quite late in the evening. Don't I, dear?" His wife nodded weakly. "She knows how it is. Incidentally, old boy," he paused a moment, struck by the novelty of his own thoughts, "do you know the Goldwaters? An accountant in this little city of ours. And very good with figures they are indeed." Again he stopped to admire the virtue of his idea, pausing once more before his final confirmation, "yes, indeed." Then without warning he turned to his daughter who sat stiffly beside David. She drew back towards her lover as though she was dodging a blow. Mary Gillespie collected the glasses and placed them neatly on the tray as her husband dashed headlong towards his goal. There wasn't a forward to match him in the county.

"You know, Deirdre, young Peader Murphy called to see you last week. Said he'd love to talk to you again. Told us what a great time you'd had together last Christmas at the his firm's party. Belle of the ball you were, to use his very words. Not that we were surprised to hear that, were we dear?" He bulldozed onwards, his tall figure shimmering in the light coming through the French windows. "Have you seen his new automobile, quite a motor I can tell you? A Jaguar, or was it a Riley? Smashing job, he'll have all the girls running after him in that machine. Know the car, David? You'll have seen it around I'm sure. Seems to have settled down in his father's outfit. An excellent firm of solicitors. If ever you need a firm of solicitors get Murphy. His father and his grandfather before him built up that firm. Plenty of good connections is what you need these days. So many fly-by-nights about! You have to be on the look out. Isn't that right, Deirdre?"

No one moved as Dermot Gillespie, finishing his address, reached for the tray to reward himself with a large whiskey.

"What's life like up at the bin, Deirdre?" Mother, feeling the ball had been passed to her, seized the opening. "It is surely time you left there and came to work for your father. He'd love to have you, wouldn't you, dear?" Seeing her husband drawing breath she rushed to make the most of her chance. "That's a gloomy place for a lovely young girl such as yourself. What you need, dear, is to settle down and get married. A woman needs security and children of her own. Before you know it you'll be on the shelf. They won't be baying at your heels then, I can tell you, my proud lady."

Mr Gillespie, not to be denied, and refreshed from his short break on the touchline, grabbed the ball.

"Wasn't that other young fellow, Sean Grady, phoning again last Friday night?"

"Oh yes dear, indeed he was." The passing movement, though, was broken into by Tom, as Deirdre silently pleaded with her brother to come to her rescue.

Coughing loudly, the young Gillespie called out. "I heard you had a good tip down at Tralee. The bookies must have been skint. Nearly all the lads at Corrigans had a few bob on him."

"Grady is one of the biggest farmers around these parts. Isn't that right, Tom?" Skilful interception was another of Dermot's highly praised achievements on the pitch.

His son had stood up and was making his farewells to his sister and David. "Off to meet the girlfriend now. Be seeing you all soon I hope. Sorry I can't stay for the meal."

Dermot Gillespie, who took the interruption in his stride, was about to continue when his wife broke in, and with a weak smile announced that lunch was ready to be served. She indicated the whereabouts of the claret and her husband set about uncorking a few bottles. His dexterity at this task was better know to his intimate friends than to the general public.

David hummed tunelessly to himself.

"If you're Irish, come into the parlour
There's a welcome there for you
If your name is Timothy or Pat
As long as you come from Ireland
There's a welcome on the mat."

Never thought of that as a racist song till now. One of my Dad's favourites at Christmas time. He closed his eyes in silent prayer. Please God, get us to hell out here. Free your people from persecution. Even a few plagues on this house would be welcome. Don't bother with the firstborn, just slay the parents. Locust, you say? That will do nicely.

He waited for an answer. Looking up to heaven, aware that Deirdre was eyeing him suspiciously, David addressed his

Maker as they went through to the dining room, and sat down at the imposing table with its twelve soldier-like satinwood chairs arranged around it. The meal began with the barley soup. David was relieved to escape behind its steamy broth. Bridie removed the bowls and laid the plates out for her employer to serve the thickly carved slices of beef. Brussel sprouts and roast potatoes. Little was said during the meal.

Two seconds to cut the over-cooked meat. What would the poor animal think to see its best end abused? Three seconds to chew each mouthful, say four mouthfuls, that's twelve seconds plus breathing time. David looked across the table to see how Deirdre was doing. The cheese's coming. It must be well matured. Probably churned as we sat here. Time goes so slow. A piece of gorgonzola and a few sachets of processed cheese wrapped in silver paper. What would Mary look like covered in asylum cream, I wonder?

"Well- it's nice to have met you, David." Mary Gillespie stood on her doorstep, sheltering behind her husband, who spoke in a concerned voice to their departing guest.

"Back to Dublin soon, I suppose, then off to England, no doubt? They need doctors over there, especially psychiatrists." His smile announced his next witticism. "Don't we send them all our mad people; getting them off to England, I'm told, is put down as a cure, isn't that right, Deirdre?"

Mother and father turned belatedly to their daughter. "We'll see you soon. Don't forget what your Mammy said to you, will you dear?"

Hallelujah! He had passed out of the land of Egypt. Didn't God tell Moses that he would free the Hebrews from bondage. David, hearing the heavy oak door close behind them, gave a small jump for joy.

"Let's get back to the asylum before we go mad," he joked, but Deirdre was not smiling.

David looked in the mirror, and felt as he had done before, that he was seeing the reflection of his father. Nodding to his image he stepped back a few paces then forward again.

"What is it about Jews that upsets people so much? Since I had dinner at your parents' house I seem to look more Semitic than before." Deirdre looked sadly across at her lover. "They let you know you were not the number one choice for their daughter. Maybe they want to send you back to the Tzars."

She threw him a cloth. "Here, wipe up the spilt cream on that chair with this. It'll remind you of better days."

When David left the house, she watched his hesitant progress as he made his way to work. Putting on a coat she slipped out through the back door and hurried towards the Church. It was her first visit since she arrived at the asylum.

She lit a candle. Thinking she was alone she knelt down in front of the altar and prayed.

"Blessed Ita of Killeedy, I've read that they tried to fit you up with an arranged marriage to some noble stallion, so you'll understand my plight. You had a thirst for something better, the same as myself. It's not the flesh I worship, although my lad's not a bad kisser when all's said and done. No, it's the spirit I've fallen for."

Deirdre looked appealingly up at the figure of Christ — arms open — looking sadly down on her from His cross, then lowered her head and continued her prayer.

"Not exactly the Divine Love the angels fixed you up with, but you'd appreciate that I'm smitten better than any of those male saints. He can't help his religion, can he now? And we're all God's children when the chips are down. Why didn't they invent a female God, then we might expect some real Christian charity down here on earth?" She looked up once more to the statue of Jesus. "A word in your ear, my Lord. Didn't all your pals run away when you were arrested, so a lot of that stuff they go on about is just propaganda to bad-mouth the Jews with. Illusions born out of prejudice."

"Well, isn't this a strange thing."

Jumping to her feet Deirdre faced the towering figure of the priest who had so recently reached out to her for comfort. Now, in her distressed state of mind, she staggered in his direction, arms poised to embrace him. He looked a picture of composure and strength.

"Are you alright, Deirdre? You don't look your old self since you moved in to that house. Can I get you anything, my dear?"

"Well I was going to ask for a miracle," she drew back, "so the cup of tea, I presume, that you have in mind for me, seems just a little bit of a let down, if you don't mind me saying so." She shook her head and was about to leave when the priest reached out to stop her.

'You seem very disappointed in me, or is it that you're angry with everybody because of the way they are reacting to your moving in with David?

"I fear my lover will be driven out by the very people he wants to belong to. You above all should see that he is needed here." Deirdre, inches from her adversary, shouted her accusation. "Wasn't it you that were the first to try and interest him in helping us, and that not more than a few months back." She wrinkled up her nose. "The smell from that uniform of yours almost had me back in childhood, just now, believing those religious fairytales your lot are so good at telling. They sow the seeds of superstition early when the night shadows make us fearful of the gremlins and we've little chance of thinking things out for ourselves. Don't they?"

"So why come here then?"

Her eyes blazing with anger she pointed to the altar. "Fuck the church. I'm here to talk to God!" She moved away from the Fintan. "It's hard to fight a war when the enemy is everywhere, even in your own home. Didn't we all think it would be different here in our asylum? It was and maybe even is different, but there is something more powerful than all of us breaking through those walls. Something more powerful than our own resolve. A deluge of deceit that has gathered strength from hypocrites and frightened do-gooders. I thought David was a bit off his rocker, going on about it all the time, but I see things differently now. The plague is narrow-mindedness and bigotry. Look at you!" She pointed accusingly at the priest. "A victim if ever there was, and yet you seem seduced by the same disease as the rest of them."

Fintan shook his head. "No, it's not true," he hesitated, "but I'm thinking that fellow of yours is a lucky man, Deirdre, to have you on his side." He studied her eyes as though seeking for a way to neutralize her sting. "I'll try not to let either of you down but without your despised miracle I need the time to catch up with real life." He kissed her forehead, glancing towards the door as he did so. "Give me time, that's all I ask."

"Tonight, my dear, you are my Indian servant. I sit here on the veranda; very pukka sahib I think you will agree." David clapped his hands twice. Taking his sun glasses from their case he pointed with them out of the window of their asylum dwelling. "See the tea plantation! How it stretches for miles till it meets the horizon."

He slipped the glasses on then reached for his drink. "Gin and tonic, ice and lemon. Straw hat placed casually on the cane chair and of course my white flannel trousers with the M.C.C. press, from the same tailors as Compton and Edrich. It's not just winning but how it's done. Mr Harold Pinter and Mr Samuel Becket knew the score and how to play the googly. Then we must prepare for the struggle. Essential gear of matching cotton short sleeved shirt must be carefully ironed to remove the creases. This is pukkah sahib regulation gear. Groomed you may guess at the fully accredited public school. No, not quite Eton. A trite more modest perhaps, Stowham and Mockelstoe, Pretty good show all the same."

David stood up and swished the bamboo cane that he had taken in from their garden. "Jolly old riding crop, prefects knew their value in the good old days and the fags knew exactly what was what. Absolutely compulsory out here. Keeps the natives in line, you know, always handy if you go riding." Walking up and down he gave the cushion on the settee a couple of sharp cracks with his crop. "Just practice strokes, don't you know, my dear. Don't worry about a thing. If you need a good solicitor get Murphy. Off you go now and let's see what you can do." Giving the cushion a few more swipes he sat down again.

"Down the hatch with the G and T. Jolly cunning these natives, what." As the room grew darker David, looking out to see the light from a full yellow moon vying with hospital lamps that hung suspended from their almost invisible posts outside his window. Sitting motionless in his chair he sipped from the glass until it was empty.

He caught his breath as Deirdre entered the room. She had darkened her face and her eyes, like large white discs stared out at him as they had done the first time he had seen her. Around her body, accentuating its outline, she had wrapped herself in a silken sari-like garment. With each movement she made as she walked towards him the robe parted to reveal the shapeliness of her long legs. Her feet were bare and she had painted her toenails a bright red.

"Oh, Memsahib, it is I who am deeply honoured by your regal presence."

She bowed her head as she stood before him. "Anything you command, my noble Highness, I shall obey. This is the custom in our great country in the presence of one, such as yourself, from the most noble island that has taught us so much we need to know of the ways of gracious gentility."

She curtsied slightly then stood before him, her eyes cast downwards. "I am but a lamb at your feet, noble gentleman."

"Jolly fine, jolly fine, my dear." He turned away from her gaze once more into the darkness outside. "But I am afraid there are one or two reports from certain quarters. Most humbly sorry. Most jolly sorry, my dear. Duty is duty you understand. God and country and all that. We have been plagued by pests for so very long. What a pity though," he muttered to himself, "such a fine gel."

Reaching out he drew aside her skirt.

"Not your fault, is it?"

"Still," he straightened up, dropping his hands to his sides as he jumped to attention in front of her. "Got to keep the natives in their place, don't you know."

"Sir Terence Fitzwilliam has especially commanded me through his esteemed accountants — the Goldwaters, of course — to keep the natives in order."

With each cut of the crop he recited the name of one of the ten plagues.

"Malchut
Yesod
Hod
Netzach
Tiferet
Gevura
Chesed
Bina
Chochma
Keter"

David threw the bamboo *(the angels are rejoicing at your freedom)* from him as their two bodies came together in pain. Both crying out as one voice in the wilderness of their own private sense of injustice, clawing at each other searching to find the real enemy.

Hassidic law demanded that insult and shame be borne silently, for, it says, when a man dies what becomes of his honor? But that was before the Six Days War.

Exhausted they slept in each other's arms on the floor of stone, lightly protected by the worn carpet that had seen better days. As he closed his eyes the Jew thought, that through his fading senses, he had glimpsed the face of the priest staring at them through the window.

Nellie Collins loaded the kitchen sink with the dirty dishes and wine glasses she had found scattered all over the place. Up to her elbows in warm suds she wallowed, bathing each item with a tenderness she might have reserved for her lost child. Through the window in front of the sink the early morning sun wrapped her in a warm glow of approval. Nellie hummed. A moment's tranquillity that no manufactured medicine could match. Her task finished, she returned to the sitting room, collecting the last of the empty wine bottles. One stood alone on the sideboard. Staring for a minute at its foreign label she tipped it into the black plastic bag together with the scattered pages of the Manchester *Guardian* that lay on the floor near the fireside chair. She was tidying copies of the B.M.J. into a neat pile when Deirdre entered the room. The two women stared at each other for a moment.

"Do you want me to leave, Miss?" Nellie looked around for her bag.

"Don't go, Nellie. I'm very glad you came early so we could meet. Do let me help you with this mess." Deirdre hurriedly gathered up some of the clothes that lay scattered about the floor and placed them in a pile at the bottom of the staircase.

When she returned, Nellie had started putting the dishes away. Deirdre checked to see if any article of her clothing still lay hidden in the room, relieved to have the opportunity of being spared any cause for further embarrassment.

On her way to the kitchen she picked up the pile of journals stacked on the sideboard and laid them in the book-case. The journal at the top of the pile was opened at a full page of advertisements for junior psychiatric positions in London mental hospitals. David had marked two of the posts with a red pen.

"Do you feel alright, Miss Gillespie? You look very pale. You're not being sick are you?" She went towards Deirdre, who waved her back.

"No, Nellie, I'm not feeling sick, not the way you mean at any rate." She grinned broadly. "But if I was, it wouldn't worry me that much. Maybe times are changing a little."

"You won't see much change from this window." Nellie nodded to the scene she had been observing. I've been looking out at this view for so long that I've almost forgotten there's a whole different world outside."

She turned to face Deirdre. "You're a strong woman, if you don't mind me saying so, Miss. Seeing you here makes me feel that I should have been a bit more courageous and think of moving on myself, before it's too late." She continued to stare at the young woman in front of her. "I suppose I was only your age when it all happened."

She turned back to the dishes. "It must be twenty years now since my brothers put me in this place. I'll not hear anything against Saint Elba's, mind, but maybe I need a change." Picking up the tea-towel she began to dry the cutlery that lay on the draining board. "You are very beautiful, Miss, everyone says so, but I can see that you have an adventurous spirit as well. When I think back to my own youth I realise that I could have been attractive, if I'd stopped to think about myself. Maybe it's youth itself that makes women so attractive. What I lacked was your courage." Nellie had turned so that her tears could not be seen. She wiped her eyes. "Me and my friend, Finoola, watch things from our window, but that's all we do, is watch."

Deirdre went over and put her arm around the older woman. "Thank you, Nellie for what you said about me. I'll try to remember it when I'm feeling down. If you do decide you need any help from me, I'd be proud to look around for you. I hear they have started to open hostels for people who want to make a new life for themselves when they leave places like this. It's been hard for women in this country, but it's time we started to help each other. People laugh at all the rumpus the young are making, but it's them that will start things changing, even if the benefits aren't seen until their own daughters go out into the world."

"You're very generous, Miss Gillespie." Nellie purred, engulfed once again in that blanket of warmth, she wanted to rub herself, like a cat might, against the radiant body of the younger woman. "I can understand what you are saying but I must be off now." She picked up her leather bag. "I'll leave a pot of strong tea for you and the Doctor before I go."

Later that evening Finoola moved her chair beside Nora's as the two woman kept watch through their observation post on the ward. She tried to sound casual.

"What's going on in the locum's house? Did you ever know the likes. Brazen hussy. Her mother will have something to say."

Getting no response she went on in the same off hand tone. "That young doctor seems to be upsetting everyone."

Nellie looked straight ahead.

"Though I hear he's a nice enough fellow."

Still getting no reaction she changed track. "Did you see them all going off to the afternoon meetings again. Maybe the Chief will sort it all out."

"Well, it certainly won't be the Superintendent. He'll be off on some little trip or other." She leaned over towards her friend. "I heard from one of the young nurses on the rounds that Doctor Reilly was angry with the locum because he was a bit late for the morning parade."

"He's got a nerve, he has, and him only worried about skiving off himself."

Finoola sat back in her chair, resigned to wait until her friend was ready to spill the beans.

Deirdre hurried back from work to find David already at home. She kissed him and went upstairs to change. When she came down he was slumped into a chair, his head buried in the *Evening Herald*. She glared at him for a minute then shouted. "If you look at that newspaper any longer it will disintegrate. Have you nothing better to do with your time than sit around like a sack of potatoes? There's no fire in the grate so what's the sense in sticking yourself in that chair for half the day. Anyone would think you had no work to do."

"Oh yes, I've plenty of work! Sign here, doctor. Press this button, doctor. Ten minutes would do the lot." David raised his paper to show Deirdre what he was reading as she stood glaring at him from the doorway. "This is work anyway. The hard going alters the form of most of these nags so I need all my powers of concentration to pick a winner. I've discovered that talking horses have great powers."

"Winners, is it?" She was unmoved. "You're more and more like those bodies in the asylum stuck under their blankets; spoon-fed addicts grasping at straws. They, at least, have the excuse that life offers them little alternative."

Exasperated she stamped her foot. "Soon you'll stick an arm out to catch the Wills' Woodbines." Deirdre paused for a moment, hands on hips. "I know what you are thinking." She moved closer to the sagging figure in the chair and pointed out in the direction of the wards. "I suppose you believe they are all victims of prejudice as well."

David stood up and tossed his newspaper to the ground. "As a matter of fact, my darling, I do believe that some of them have been put away because people could not deal with their difference. And I'm not altogether alone in those beliefs. I suppose you could never imagine the possibilities for revolutionary potential in Vini's position. Look what Gandhi was able to achieve, and him under a blanket. If we don't have politics our rights will be stolen from us."

Eyes blazing, she shouted back at him. "Very funny. You are supposed to be helping them, not joining them." Turning to leave, she mocked. "OK I'll come and visit you twice a day to see how you are getting on. Oh, and I'll remember to throw the Wills' Woodbines in your direction. No doubt you'll find more agreeable companionship with Vini and his like." She ignored his grin. "Another psychiatrist bites the dust by over identifying with his patients."

As she spoke Fintan entered the sitting room.

"Is it safe to come in here? I knocked and got no answer, so as the door was unlocked I took the liberty of entering." He looked from one to the other. "You both look ready to explode. That's not going to help anyone, is it?" The Priest shut the door behind him. "Why don't we go out a bit." He brightened at his own suggestion. "We could go to the sea, couldn't we? A bit of ozone in the lungs and possibly a pint or two." He looked at David then back to Deirdre, then shook his head sadly. "I wish I could help but maybe you'd rather I make myself scarce."

As he moved towards the door David called after him. "The two of you should take yourselves off and leave me to wallow in my own misery."

Deirdre turned on her lover shouting. "What's going on in that warped mind of yours, David? No, on second thoughts, don't bother telling me. I can't say it matters. I'll get my coat and Fintan and me will be off down to Mulligan's for a jar. If you change your mind you can follow us, but don't take it out in those trees again for God's sake. We don't want you turning yourself into a victim yet again, do we?"

Without waiting for a reply she took the priest's arm and headed towards the car. They ordered their pints and took them to a small corner table. Mulligan himself was preoccupied with the news broadcast on Radio Eireann. He'd heard every story his clients had to tell at least four times. His love affair with the radio; the antidote.

"Has he given up on us I wonder?" Fintan spoke with a certain relish, the creamy foam of the Guinness settling on his upper lips. "It's not long till he'll be away. Not long at all." He wiped the back of his hand across his lips with all the gusto of a fellatio king who had just drunk his cup full. "I can't decide if he's deserting us or if it is us that are letting him down."

The priest unexpectedly reached out to grab hold of Deirdre's hand. She quietly freed herself from his grasp and sank back into her chair without making any other comment, but glanced nervously around the room before she replied. "So you think he will leave me, do you? You're probably right. Since I took him home to visit my parents I've felt him draw back into himself." Gritting her teeth. "I'm not letting go that easily. I've had more from him in the few months he's been here than from all the hunt balls and the like that my mother set up for me. Anyway I have to think of my own future as well and I won't be spending my whole life here, that's for certain." Fintan edged his chair a little nearer. "It's lucky for them that can leave, but what about the ones that need to stay? Let's hope those remaining don't get left with the feeling that they're just discards. Sometimes great drama can be easier to manage than the steady everyday support. Perhaps that's why Wilfred, Eileen, Sarah and the others wanted to get back to their routines when all the excitement invested in my problems dies down."

Deirdre leaned towards the priest when he had finished speaking. "There's a lot in what you say."

He moved his head closer to her. The perfumed intimacy intoxicated him. Dizzy, he laboured to catch his breath ...

Back in the darkened room. He could hear, even smell, the nurse as she chanted her spellbinding secret code.

Deirdre was asking. "What about yourself and Eileen then? You're more than brother and sister from what I've seen, and I'm not referring to what went on between us all at Will's place." She whispered her question.

Fintan shifted uncomfortably in his seat. Intoxicated, but not by drink, the glass of stout pushed to one side. His head spinning, he struggled to concentrate on Deirdre's voice and managed a response.

"Eileen's a wonderful woman, and I'd be lost without her. She has been more a mother to me and God knows I needed that. A lady of great passions, and she seemed to understand what ailed me. It was her that told the Chief about my troubles, for which I'll be eternally grateful."

The words that spilled out seemed to be his but he felt divorced from their meaning. Without warning the priest clasped Deirdre's head to him and hurriedly kissed her on the lips. As she struggled to free herself from his grasp she felt his hand moving on her thigh beneath the table, searching under her skirt until his fingers had poked their way into her startled body. Paralysed she sat staring at the man who was silently abusing her, afraid if she spoke her voice would betray her. Taking her passivity for acquiescence his hand moved in a grotesque caress as it slowly explored between her thighs.

Lesley Mulligan, only daughter in a litter of a dozen children, took her father's place behind the counter. It was more the silence than any sound that made her look up from her comic. As she did so she caught sight of the priest's habit as he dashed out into the night.

Then she turned to see the lone figure at the table stagger to her feet, knocking over a glass, as she made her escape.

"Is everything all right, Miss Gillespie?" She called out after her disappearing customer.

Deirdre locked herself in her car, crying out in anger, her hands clasped to the wheel, undecided as to what to do. Who could she turn to? She sat for some time staring out of the window before starting the car up. About a mile down the road she saw Fintan's hunched figure walking along the verge. Without hesitation she drew up along side him and lowered the window. Keeping her foot on the accelerator, she shouted out. "You bastard, I should run you down. You're nothing more than an animal."

The priest stumbled forward and threw himself down in front of the car. For a moment she let her foot rest on the accelerator revving the engine as she did so. Then abruptly she pulled on the hand brake, jumped out on to the road leaving the car door open. "Get up you big fool, I knew you were ignorant, but I never thought you were stupid." She leaned over his body and roughly grabbed him, between his legs, through his trousers. "Do you find that sexy? I'm damned sure you don't and neither do I! Grow up for God's sake." She stood up. "On your feet before someone comes along."

She put an arm out to help him, all the time trying to remind herself that the part she played in the priest's treatment might make him believe that she desired him in a different way. "If I didn't know you were a decent man I'd kick you where you lie, but if I resist the urge don't go thinking I'm one of those women who makes a hero out of some cowardly bully who beats the living daylights out of her."

He sat beside her in the car looking away from her as she drove home. The Priest suddenly turned towards her. His voice croaked.

"You won't say anything to David, will you?" He was weeping. "I'm not that different from Father Tom, am I?" He saw that his words were having little effect on his tight lipped victim. "I know it's asking a lot of anyone to understand why I'm so fucked up. It's worse now that I can't really turn to David for help again. I've abused the woman he's in love with."

Getting out of the car, as they drew up outside his house, he held the door open. "Try to forgive me. Before I met you all here I was had no hope. Now I can't get you out of my mind and I don't seem to be able to find a way to deal with that."

He shut the car door gently, leaning through the open window. His tone was suddenly harsh. "Why should he be so privileged? I'm not the only one that feels that."

He walked a few paces from the car then turned back. "Christ, Deirdre, I am fucked up, and to tell the truth I blame those sessions at the Chief's place for making me lose my bearings. Sometimes it's hard to tell which world I'm living in. At least I'm in the right place, a mental hospital, and not a Church, letting on everything is wonderful."

The house was silent as Deirdre entered. She ran herself a warm bath, sobbing quietly while waiting for it to fill. In the water she rocked backwards and forwards as she soaped her body. Later she tiptoed silently downstairs, Reaching into the cupboard for the tea-caddy, she made herself a pot of tea and sat in the dark looking out of the window. Had it been a terrible mistake to put so much trust in the Chief's ideas? Perhaps her mother was right after all.

It was almost two am when she crept into bed beside David. She tried to settle beside him but he moved restlessly, pulling the covers from her. Curled up into his shape, she tried to sooth his agitation by holding him tightly in her arms. So much had gone into developing their bonding that withdrawing from him now seemed unthinkable. It would be like killing a new-born child after she'd nurtured its growth through a stormy pregnancy.

At the other side of the asylum the priest sat over his empty fireplace, drinking his way through a bottle of whiskey. At one am he made himself a black coffee and went to the phone, dialling the Chief's number. Before it had rung he put the phone down.

Deirdre sat at the table, the events of the previous evening pounding through her head. A shudder went through her body as she recalled her response to the assault. Stifled by lassitude.

At sixteen two boys in her class had trapped her in the lavatories after a dance. One had held her hands behind her back while the other one felt her breasts through her dress while he forced a kiss on her. Stuck up bitch. They'd let her go when she screamed. She'd informed her brothers, who got together with a gang of their friends and waited for the two boys after a dance. It was the last time they tried anything like that again. The Gillespies had a reputation to keep up, she'd been told. Dermot's handsome face often graced the back pages of the *Echo* and prospective members of the Dail made sure that they were seen in his illustrious presence when elections loomed. Deirdre's friends, not blessed with such heroic parents, vied with each other to be asked to her house after school. They could not dream that she envied them their freedom from the tyranny of a life under the constant glare of public scrutiny.

When Fintan had pawed under her skirt something seemed to prevent her moving away. This puzzled her. She wrapped the dressing gown tightly around herself. There was no way she could have invited it to happen, of that she felt sure.

When David came downstairs she went to the kitchen and returned with two cups of tea. They sat, drinking in silence before Deirdre turned to him. "It's no good. I've got to tell you."

She looked at him wildly. "Promise me you'll hear the whole of what I have to say before you interrupt."

David, startled by the tone of her voice, nodded his head in agreement. He listened quietly as she began her account of what had happened in Mulligan's the previous night.

"We were talking away to each other when suddenly I felt those huge fingers of his wander slowly up my leg. I couldn't believe it was happening." She shuddered. "It was like one of those party pranks young kids play to scare each other. I even felt a bit giggly until it dawned on me that he had poked his way right inside me. Great thick spider's spinnerets, weaving a passage through me. Injecting poison into my system till my voice froze. The terrifying thing about it was that I seemed to lose all power to resist his invasion."

Deirdre looked pleadingly at David, wanting him to understand. "Like defenceless villagers who line the pavements to watch an invading army march through their streets, I could find no way to repel the advance of these clawed appendages as they moved to occupy my body."

David, unable to restrain himself any longer, jumped to his feet, yelling wildly in the direction of the priest's house. "You dirty pig. I'd never have believed you could sink that low." He hesitated then turned back to Deirdre who was weeping, her head buried in her hands. "If only I'd gone with you both, this would never have happened. I'm a fool. Hasn't the man been spying on us as we made love?"

Deirdre looked puzzled but he brushed her questions aside. "I tried to convince myself I was imagining it, but I'm certain now that it was him I saw at nights, a starved animal, staring at us through our window at us. All the time I wanted to believe it was just a trick of the light. After all he was our friend, and more. Those sessions with the Chief may have gone someway to relieving our priest from his sexual guilt but it hasn't helped him to find a way of dealing with his hunger." He flung both his arms around Deirdre again, as he shouted out "And this is the man that wanted us to help him. I'm more inclined to kick his balls in."

"You promised to hear the whole story." Deirdre shrugged off his embrace. "I followed Fintan in my car and when I finally caught up with him I came within a whisker of deliberately running him down."

David grimaced. "That wouldn't have been much help, now would it? Let us both try and calm down so that we can try and work out what should be done."

Uneasily she pointed towards the window. "He's not there now, is he?" The colour had drained from her face. "David, I want you to contact Wilfred and ask him to come over."

It would not do justice to the Chief to describe his presence as calming. Not a guru to distract anxiety with mantras and soothing words, more a warrior prepared to enter the fray and help renew the spirit of engagement.

Deirdre greeted him with a hug. Composed, she quietly related the events of the previous evening to the nurse. "When he groped me I had the impression Fintan imagined we were back in your house. I'd leaned over to ask him about Eileen and himself and I think it was the perfume that could have rekindled the atmosphere of our gatherings. It was like we were both transported to your darkened rooms, back in a trance for a few seconds."

Deirdre shuddered. "I do mean both of us. There, in Mulligan's pub, I lost all sense of what made those sessions seem positive. I felt like a prizefighter does when he abuses the discipline he has trained for and gets caught up in a pub brawl." She looked from one man to the other. "What is there to stop the same reactions being triggered off again? Have we now become simple minded lap-dogs who are prey to manipulation at any time?"

She shook her head in disbelief. "Thank God it was you, Wilfred, who held the strings on those nights and not some malevolent influence."

On their way to Fintan's, Deirdre held David's hand. "We may be engaged in trying to help others but let's hope that God will help us to help ourselves. If we could find a way to deal with our own problems, and soon, I'd feel a lot more cheerful." She stopped and drew him towards her. "We must find a way of being together, you and I, that would give us real strength. Already having rows, and you looking to England for work without even telling me you were. That's really what I need you to tell me."

David looked at her angrily. "Not my choice, as you well know." He held her hand and set off again striding out briskly towards the priest's house.

Wilfred had already pushed open the front door. Calling out he made his way into the sitting room. Entering gingerly he peered around, frightened of what he might find. Then he saw the priest hunched up in a chair, his black habit drawing him into the shadows of the room, invisible to them at first. He sat immobile, seeming not to notice his visitors.

"So she told you." Hearing Fintan speak brought a sigh of relief from David.

"Yes. Deirdre told me because she had to speak to someone about it, and it's a good thing that she did."

The Chief drew the others back, and knelt down by the priest's chair. "We are all here to help you, but its not going to be easy after what's happened. I didn't bargain for this, I have to admit, and I'm not sure whether to be angry with you or to blame myself."

The nurse had moved over to the priest and embraced him, leaving one arm around Fintan's shoulder as he spoke. "Reason is emotion's slave, and don't think we can find any easy explanations for what's happened. Of course I want to believe, like Deirdre says, that the spirit of our venture was for good and that is what will rescue us, but who knows now what path our actions will take us on?"

Fintan spoke in a heavy voice. "A few hours ago I thought I was finished altogether. I know it will be hard to put things right but I have spent the whole night berating myself for letting you all down. Not just what happened at Mulligan's, but my jealousy of David." He hesitated, then blurted out "I just wanted him to go. Deirdre belongs to us, not to him, a stranger, and a Jew to boot. I started to spy on them and tried to imagine it was me making love to her, not him."

The priest grasped Wilfred's arm. "And that after me befriending him and encouraging him to help us."

David and Deirdre left the Chief with Fintan and made their way back to their house. On the way he turned to her. "Let's hope that we can hang on to the positive motives that have driven us in this endeavour. So often it is evil that seems to win out. How many people remember the couple who sheltered Anne Frank, I wonder? But Hitler's name lives on, and I bet that the echo of those jackboots his followers marched in will excite many a tin-pot dictator waiting in the wings to take a bow.'

"Well, at least we are in the battle, so those scars will be there to remind us of the dangers.

"I am beginning to make sense of what I have read of Freud's therapy. How easy it is for the healer to be drawn in by his own unconscious needs. How desperate am I to be the insider. Am I drowning in my desire? Back inside: back inside what I wonder?"

That evening David and Deirdre drove out of Dargle to the sea. Walking hand in hand without saying much for almost an hour they returned to the hospital and sat together by the open fire. As she turned to kiss him she laughed. "Threesomes don't seem to work very well, even in these days of communes and solidarity, do they my love?"

Later the same evening, the Chief rang them and fixed the time for the next gathering at his house. David knew then that the time for his biggest challenge had arrived.

Am I still a free agent in this adventure or am I imprisoned by the same dark forces that had trapped the priest.

When Deirdre left for work the next day he rang his father.

Oisin is one example of the interspecies mating. He is the son of Ronn and Sadbh but was bom to his mother when she was in a deer shape. He is destined to be in a human shape if his mother does not lick him: however, unable to refrain from one act of tenderness, she gives him one such lick on the forehead where Oisin, which means 'little deer', retains a tuft of hair

Rees Alwyn Brindly. *Celtic Tales*

The admissions officer sat at the table awaiting the new arrival. A harpsichord announced the variation on the previous gathering at the Chief's house. This time it was the Jew that stood awaiting attention, the priest the witness, while the official entered details in his book. The lights of the room were turned off as a nurse took her place beside the new arrival. Two freshly lit candles cast their shadow on the standing figures and, as the music was turned louder, the young woman announced in a stern voice.

"This man thinks he's a priest." The officer at the desk scribbled on the case notes in front of him, then signalled his colleague towards the screens standing at the opposite end of the room. David Benn felt himself guided by the nurse, floating rather than walking, and with each step he became more closely identified with the figure of the priest whose confession he had so avidly listen too barely five months previously. Unlike the earlier visit to the candlelit drama, when he had struggled to avoid succumbing to the hypnotic atmosphere and remain an observer of events, he now rejoiced in the ease at which he was engulfed by the excitement of those around him. The priest, when he took his seat later, would see himself and his own turmoil in what was being acted out before him. The Jew knew the woman by his side was Sarah, but at that moment she had little connection to the person he had talked to on his ward rounds. Once behind the screen she began to remove his shirt, slowly drawing it over his head. He revelled in his own passivity, unconcerned about the outcome, his senses saturated with what had now become the familiar fragrance that pervaded the atmosphere. Her fingers undid the buttons of his trousers, touching his body in caressing movements.

Now she has me in her hand. Stop. No, it's too late.

I am the worker of miracles, the Druid Rabbi.

The nurse kissed his lips, gently at first, then with slow gyrating movements of her body immersed him in her caress.

"Father forgive me." She breathed her words into his mind, then stood back without taking her eyes off him. Here is your robe, Father." She slipped the white cassock over his head, and led him out. He was no longer the observer.

As he was guided from behind the screens into the candlelit inner sanctum, his own identity was smothered by the images of Father Tom, each movement a resurrection generated from Fintan's soulful tale. Now he strutted, proudly bowing to the assembled congregation.

"Get their clothes off, cousin. In the name of all that's holy. I'll teach them a thing or two, see if I don't. Come on, cousin Fay, it's time those foundlings were taught a lesson. They are lucky to have a roof over their heads. We'll see that they love, honour and obey, by God we will."

Moving closer to the nurse by his side he reached out to grope her body. "How did you get here, Mary, my dear sister? Never mind, just come over to me. A little kiss, eh, and what about that son of yours? All he needs is educating a wee bit, a few facts of life, eh sister?"

Sarah reached out to remove the robe and then slowly lead the ranting figure towards the bed and lay him face down across it. Fintan Dunbar, who had been ushered into the room by the Chief, was seated in the same chair that David had occupied when he had been the witness. He sat, his grim features focused intently on the events unfolding before him in the darkened room. Suddenly he rose from the chair as though to interrupt the proceedings, but then sat back, his unsmiling eyes fixed on the body stretched across the bed. Every gesture he had beheld in those few moments evoked the priest's contempt for his uncle. The sounds of the rod wielded by his hated relative echoed in his head, as did the cries of the tiny victims. The Jew's every gesture evoked the aura of false piety engraved in the priest's memory as he had watched his Uncle Tom caress his mother. Each action cloyed to Fintan's senses, feeding the venom that urged him to lunge forward and strangle his enemy. Instead he slumped back in his chair as he beheld the scenes that manacled him to his tortured past. Eileen Fahy raised the whip above the passive figure on the bed. She brandished the lash with a gusto that brought cries of anguish as it cut into its target. Fintan Dunbar's own body winced in unison with the writhing victim on the bed. He felt the restraining hand of the Chief on his shoulder, as once more he struggled with waves of outraged emotion that threatened to engulf him. Flourishing the whip for its final act, the torturer scourged her victim with renewed resolve, then threw the instrument of pain onto the floor, while the slim figure of Deirdre materialized from the darkness. Moving ghostlike from the ether, she cast her net, drawing those observing into its hypnotic web. Fintan repeated his Uncle's name under his breath and gripped the Chief's arm tightly, struggling to keep afloat.

Deirdre, turned the tortured figure over. Mounted, she gripped him tightly with her naked limbs. Spasmodically her thighs began to move. He lay beneath her, arms outstretched as her excitement impelled her movements, rhythmically back and forwards. His wincing form strained to feed her own excitement. She was Saint Teresa's Vision of Ecstasy on her mission, reuniting flesh and spirit. Celibacy was undone. The spirit of the Cross rejoined with the feelings of mortal flesh. Deirdre drew back stretching her arms wide as in some victory salute, before slithering down to rest on the floor at the feet of the injured figure. Burying her head in his loins she sucked the substance from them, and as before, anointed the man with his own semen, then rubbed her hands, wet with the holy fluid of real life, over her own body.

"My judgments are to be respected, not discussed, sayeth the Lord, for they are beyond the comprehension of the human mind." The priest recited the psalm to himself as he shifted fearfully in his chair. He felt that he should rise up to condemn the secular blasphemy that gave credence to the scenes he had witnessed. He, more than any in the room, understood the meaning of the grotesque drama that had unfolded before him, yet he feared to claim his right to such a freedom that brazenly endeavoured to unlock the secrets of his suffering. That right of understanding the nature of the deeds that moulded his life. Surely this was beyond the powers of mere mortals who were condemned to seek salvation though a blind repetition of pain. But now he was a witness to the blueprint that had shaped his life

No longer the simple tragic figure of the asylum priest, the Jew lay where Deirdre had left him, his consciousness swamped by an excitement that elevated him beyond that earthly being. He had left these shores to search in deeper waters. Oblivious of pain, the images he pursued threatened to confiscate all judgment. Imagination, that had been his greatest strength, now imperilled his reason. What had ensured his freedom dragged him now towards a heavenly kingdom. In his grasp the ultimate prize of union with their Saviour.

Each thought gripped him as a new enlightenment that glorified its importance beyond all worldly measure. Uncertainty no longer anchored his aspirations as exhilaration made him a prisoner of illusory freedom.

Fintan Dunbar , wrestling to maintain his reason, watched, as those about him, stood dazzled by the vision that was their own creation. They gazed in worship of the crumpled figure oblivious of the earthly glory in themselves. Those who bravely risked the ridicule of the world outside the walls of the asylum, wailed in ecstatic self abasement. The torment of divine adoration at the image of the saviour they had invented to serve themselves, now seduced them from their senses.

Only the priest heard Deirdre call out the Jew's name.

"David! David!"

The words were absorbed into a cauldron of sensations that impinged on the elated soul of her lover, just one more incomprehensible element in the sea of his confusion. She whispered his name again, her lips pressed closer to his ear. "David! David!"

He did not heed her words. Instead, it was her heated breath that was sucked into his head, to feed the fervour that rocketed to dreams of unity with a world he'd longed to enter.

As Deirdre spoke she shook his body, frantically trying to rouse him. He explored the heavens from his high rock: her actions dragged him from his safe haven and threatened to plunge him into an abyss. He shrugged her off.

Heroic explorer sailing to his Byzantium stood in the warmth of Gods Holy fire.

Who was this forbidden creature intruding on His Holy Mountain? He, who would not be denied.

Abruptly, as if douched by a shower of icy water, Deirdre's now harsh tone began to penetrate his mind.

"Jewman!" Her stony voice flung the words at him. She only understood their weight.

"Jewman!"

"Jewman!"

"Jewman!" The gunshot, that everyday could puncture his delusion of belonging now shot down his soaring balloon. Travelling with speed it struck the very heart of his elation. David turned as though to hit out at her as she battled with the monster that had usurped his mind.

Fintan sprung from the chair he'd been rooted to, catching the Doctor as he fell forward on his face. Eileen and Sarah, reunited with their temporal strengths, helped raise him gently to his feet, as Deirdre stepped once more into the shadows. An airship, out of air, had landed.

David allowed himself to be led him back to the room where his admission had taken place, before he was assisted from the house. When they had departed, the Chief emerged from the shadows in the place he had watched over his creation. He stood for a while thinking about his visit to Father Joseph. Then he blew out the candles and collapsed exhausted into the chair that had been occupied by Fintan.

David gripped the arms of the two nurses who supported him as they made their way slowly back to his house in the asylum grounds. "Hold on tight to me now. Maybe the angels were keeping an eye on things and helped me find my place, if only to avoid confusing the doorman at those pearly gates."

"Man can embody truth but he cannot know it."

William Butler Yeats

The following morning Fintan entered the doctor's house by the back door. He found Sarah asleep, curled up in a fireside chair. She breathed deeply, through half open lips, her hands folded across her breasts. He stood over her watching each movement of her body.

Unexpectedly she opened her eyes and jumped to her feet. "Dead to the world. I hope you haven't had too long a wait." Her gaze fixed on his as she smoothed down her creased clothes.

The priest shook his head. "Don't worry, my dear, Wilfred told me he'd left the back door open. He'll be along with Deirdre any time now."

Sarah glanced in the mirror above the fireplace. Both hands swept through her dishevelled hair; unwanted thoughts brushed away. Then she bent to poke the ashes of last night's fire. What would her parents think on their way to Church, if they knew? As the embers glowed she quickly added kindling and stood back as the wood burst into flame.

When she turned to the priest, who stood but a hair's breath away, he quickly stepped back. From the foot of the stairs she murmured, more to herself than to the cleric. "He must have slept soundly, for I haven't heard a peek out of him all night." Then louder. "You look after that fire and I'll put the kettle on as soon as I've given the Doctor a call. He'll want to know you're here." Sarah scurried up to David's bedroom. Hesitant, she tiptoed to the bed and looked down at the sleeping figure. Why had she been so angry with him? Before shaking him out of his slumber she leaned over to kiss the young man briefly on his lips.

David, unshaven and pale, joined them. "I've been dreaming. No, it was more than a dream.

The journey through time had actually happened. I've been on the mount, a time traveller who has brought back knowledge of a previous existence in history. I visited my ancestors. But have I got the proof that I am one of them? Look at my betting slip. The bet? It covers the multitude of possibilities. All my family are on the docket. Members of my tribe, from the hoards who gathered in caves in ancient times. Drawn from my genes, out through history. Peas in a pod. Irishmen and women– remember we climbed the mount together. Knowing each other through knowing oneself. To be Christ, I'd only to suspend my consciousness and draw on knowledge that gave us common ground. My Judaism for one. I've mingled with ghosts who had regained their existence by slipping in and out of other ghosts or haunted the living to discover their own selves. Is this what fucking is really about; the inside story, a sort of DNA test? Looking for lost parts of ourselves. And our priest? He too has gleaned a new knowledge – unwanted before – of a self that dwelt in his Uncle. Knowledge, like castor oil, good for you but not too palatable.

"Thanks for looking after me, Sarah. Stay with us, won't you? There'll be a great deal to talk over when the others arrive. We're all in this together after all."

"I don't think you'll be needing me now, Doctor, and besides I have lots to do on the wards." The nurse blushed as she saw the young doctor staring at her while she made the tea. Her adventures were rooted in thoughts that would fill her mind on ward rounds. She had stored up sufficient for her needs. The secret was not only about how to switch on, but when to switch off. Others must go further for their fulfilment. This was her stop.

Fintan crouched over the fire trying to light his cigarette as the door closed quietly behind Sarah. His hands shook forcing him to throw away the remains of the match as it burnt its way towards his fingers. Wilfred arrived with Deirdre and Father Joseph, who withdrew into the background after he'd been introduced to the doctor. Fintan stood up, edging toward the young woman. He grasped awkwardly at her hand, holding onto it as though it was some fragile object he feared to damage. All the while he searched for a signal from her that would instruct him as to what he should do or say next.

Deirdre's tone was sharp. "Come now, man, try and let go a bit. You have no pretensions to keep up here anymore than the rest of us. Surely be to God we've got past that stage at least." Glaring, first at the way he held her in his massive hand and then in disgust at the vapid expression on his face, she shouted "Stop trying to pretend you are treating me like I'm some sort of rare and delicate blossom." She withdrew her hand from the priest.

"Be patient with me, will you." Fintan drew back in his chair. Striking the match, firmly this time, he lit his cigarette and puffed silently on it for a few moments.

"There are not many I've met that measure up to the like of yourself." He examined her through the smoke then pitched the cigarette into the grate. "You want me to say it and I will." His voice rose in anger. "I'm not that different from my uncle or anyone else who is cut off from their natural instincts. The man I've hated most is not that different from myself. I'll learn that now and I'll learn to live with it. The bait the Holy orders use to entice us to fit their image had me hooked and but for all of you I'd still be addicted." He looked appealingly towards his two friends, then withdrew back into himself for a few moments before turning again to Deirdre. Father Joseph, who had stepped forward between them, addressed Fintan. "You'll still have our support. We know that everyone wants us priests to be saints, even ourselves."

Deirdre shook her head impatiently. "Do try and understand, Fintan, what I'm trying to do now is to get you to look at me, and I can see that you do not like to do that very much. Am I speaking too loud for you maybe?"

Deirdre stood up, flung her arms down in disgust and glared first at Fintan and then at the others in the room. "Please don't look away. Can't you see that I am battering my way out of my own prison; my female identity as prescribed by you men."

David stretched uncomfortably in his chair. Reaching forward with the fire tongs he delivered a few carefully chosen lumps of coal to the fire. When he turned back, Deirdre was still standing glowering down at him.

"There's enough heat in me without that. I have not taken part in all this just to have the value of our adventure demeaned." She tossed her head in the direction of the fire then stood very still. Momentarily lost in reverie she seemed to look beyond the men in the room. No longer engaged in mockery of the sad figure of the priest or her bemused lover who sat before her. It was the centuries of misogyny, supported by the Church, that had become her opponent. It was that which had cast its spell over her sex and entrapped her own mother in its seductive claws. This was the monster she faced and she had spared no device in her battle to defeat it.

"Do I sound ugly?" She shouted the words into the room startling her listeners. "I hope so. Men have made a woman's point of view into an ugly thing. That is what you need to know." Then taking a step towards the downcast figures seated before her, she spoke quietly. "I'm no sacrificial lamb, so spare me your guilt. Perhaps its pride we should be feeling and not shame, for having the temerity to enter the fight."

"If that's the case there won't be many that will share our admiration." David lifted a copy of the previous day's *Irish Times*. "Look at this front page. Can't you see the headlines if any word of the events here ever leaked out? 'Orgy in the asylum', your picture, Deirdre, as the evil seductress. Wouldn't the vultures of respectability have a field day especially if they heard it was the Goldberg variation that was played last night. There's a whole industry out there just looking to make a scandal that will feed their prejudice. The hacker's scandal is the name it's got."

Deirdre raised her ·eyes towards heaven. "There you go again, claiming all the suffering. At least we'd both be nailed to the same cross, wouldn't we, or do you still believe that it's Jews only need apply in the suffering stakes?"

She turned to Fintan. "And please don't feel there isn't room for you on the cross. The only difference is, that having discovered they have failed to remove your balls while training you for celibacy, the hierarchy will make sure you are in protective custody while the scandal is around. Isn't there a slush fund for you lot when you get into trouble?"

David heard the two gentle knocks on the front door.

Nellie Collins entered quietly. "It's all right, Doctor, I'll not interrupt you." Looking towards Father Joseph she curtsied slightly. "It's good to see you again, Father, after all this time. I've brought all some sandwiches and a flask of coffee." Nellie placed the hamper beside Deirdre. "God bless youse all." She crossed herself in a perfunctory manner as she closed the door behind her.

David unscrewed the flask, releasing its bitter chocolate aroma into the stuffy overheated room, while Deirdre unwrapped the sandwiches. Before they began eating, she turned to the silent figures of Joseph and Wilfred. "I told Nellie I'd help her leave here if she wanted to and now I think it's time for me to move on."

As she spoke David went to her and put his arm around her shoulder. Wilfred was the first to respond. "I'm relieved to hear you say so, Deirdre. To tell the truth we had not reckoned on the force of our play. Our healer sucked in through the power of his own cravings. It was you that helped to break the spell and bring him back to earth. None of us had known how far a dream could carry us and without moving physically. To say I underestimated the danger we found ourselves in is an understatement in itself. We've all had adventures beyond our dreams. Our healer had his own dreams beyond anything that we imagined."

Fintan shifted uncomfortably. "They say people commit murder for love. I suppose I can understand that, but isn't it a strange sort of emotion that drives a child into the skin of the person he hates most in the whole world in order to keep his mother's love. I know that now. That's not far off a form of self annihilation."

He withdrew, sinking into a private reverie, pondering on his own thoughts.

Deirdre took the phone call from the superintendent's secretary just before she was about to set off on the short walk to her office. She had begun to enjoy the novelty of living in the hospital grounds. The unexpected summons from her boss left her feeling uneasy. Although everyone knew by this time that she was living with David, an official call for her at the locum's residence was surely no friendly acknowledgement of that fact.

Doctor Reilly beckoned her to the seat in front of his desk. For once he did not feel under pressure: there were no race meetings that day, Nevertheless he shifted uneasily under Deirdre's firm gaze. Desmond Gillespie had leaned on the doctor. A man of influence in Dargle and beyond; some hinted that he was a close friend of a well-known Republican leader. Not a person who could easily be ignored. Reilly had already been persuaded that the insulin coma ward could be called upon to offer temporary shelter for a local Scarlet Pimpernel on the run from the police. Who would dream of looking under the blankets in a room full of unconscious schizophrenics.

"I'm afraid, my dear, that I've got some bad news for you." He moved the files on his desk to one side and cleared his throat. Why, he wondered should he be put in this position? He looked at the poised figure facing him. A beauty, just as her mother had been. Hadn't he lusted after Mary in his day; only in his head, of course.

"I have to ask you to leave the hospital." He noticed that her expression did not alter. "And your job, of course."

"Is there a reason, Doctor Reilly? My work, unsatisfactory? Maybe the patients have made complaints about me?" Her voice was cold. The Superintendent cleared his throat and looked away. What could she see in that Jewboy, anyway? He was mystified. It had been a mistake to employ him. No doubt he'd filled his mind with all that rubbish from R. D. Laing, another of those psychoanalyst types with a head full of Marxist trash. No wonder the Archbishop wants to ban the books. Birds of Paradise indeed. I've been a fool, he thought, but how was I to know the trouble he'd cause. He'll be gone in a day or so, and O'Sullivan will be back from his trip to America to take his place, that's one blessing. The little man sighed. Even the Chief seemed to find Benn interesting. God knows why. He risked a quick glance at Deirdre. What could he say to her? Women have odd tastes, that's for sure. And these days they seemed to have no morals. All that hippy stuff from England and America. Too much money and not enough sense.

The superintendent's job had fallen into his lap when he'd been fortunate enough to have arranged the admission of the Archbishop's mother for him. Senile dementia was not easily cared for at home.

"Spare me your excuses." Deirdre stood up. "When a country shakes hand with the Devil it takes a long time to cleanse itself of the contagion." At the door she turned. "None of us are Saints ... not even yourself. If you faced up to that you wouldn't have to go marching about looking for scapegoats to boost your little egos."

As David walked by the Chief's house on his way home he stopped as he recognized the strident tone of Dooley's fiddle scraping out its tune. He felt its sound drawing him towards it with the power of a Pied Piper. Stopping by the gate he smiled, remembering the tune and the trips to local hotspots he had spent with Deirdre. Had Dooley found a fifth string to catch the hidden sounds that only the wandering tribes could hear? Humming to himself he walked back home.

Gra mo chroi mochroi mo chruiscin.
Slain-te geal mo vuirnin"

Approaching his own house the mood of hopelessness

returned to grip him. A cloud of despond. *Why hadn't he insisted that Deirdre had come with him to see his father? It was obvious that her parents would never take to him. A locum was little more than a gypsy to the likes of Dermot Gillespie and his lady wife.*

He entered the house through his back door. All was quiet. On the kitchen table he found a note. "I've been told to leave by Dr Reilly. Don't blame him. I'm certain that my family leant on him. I've gone to stay at a friend's. Don't go running after me because they'll be watching. Believe me, as you asked me to believe you, you'll be in danger if you do. People of influence have their thugs to do their dirty work. Just open the newspaper and you'll see them in action. I've loved you, David, and will always, Deirdre.

In the sitting room everything was neat and tidy. Upstairs the posters that she had so recently pinned to the walls had gone. He could picture her as though she was there in the room in front of him, the way it was last night.

"Couldn't we have lots of children?" she'd shouted. "Maybe they would look like you, but sure I wouldn't mind that." She knew his thoughts from the sadness in his face. In his mind it was the Gillespies, sending him to England to rejoin the wandering tribe away from the place he sought to make his home.

"Maybe it's not me you were in love with, but my country, and I've not been able to get you a season ticket." He'd tried to silence her but had failed. "They'll say I am mad if I tell them my happiest days were spent inside an asylum, won't they?"

She had moved closer, pushing him backwards with her outstretched arms until he had fallen back onto the bed behind him.

"I'll never leave you, Deirdre. I'm not crazy, yet."

Now he went to the window and looked out. The neat roads running through the gardens, almost in full bloom, were deserted. It's only me and that rat in the fuel house. Maybe she will follow me to England on Dracula's boat. At least the barman at the Grand would be pleased at that. David threw himself on the bed sniffing in Deirdre's smells.

I can smell my mother, the mother who wheeled me from Harold's Cross to Adelaide Road. She is taking her last breath. Don't let it out, there will never be another one. It will be dreary, so hang on. Don't believe that stuff about life after death. Just a trick. Nothing to be done. This is her FINAL. I gathered you up and gave you one long last lingering look to keep for ever, or rather till it is my turn. Then out into the garden with Aunts talking in everyday tones. Didn't our Robert do well in his exams and have you seen Edward's new girlfriend? That was what hardened me up to the hard man I am to-day. Then each time I went home I'd lie face down on my mother's empty bed embracing her absent body. The smells lasted for two years then drifted away. Look up and you'll see her. Some fathers know such a lot. Selecting a star was like having an eye which could look back at me.

David hugged the pillow that Deirdre's head had slept on.

Hadn't it served me well in the darkest times?

In the morning he reached out for her.

The pillow and the blankets all lay in a heap on the floor.

Downstairs he found another note, this time from the Chief.

Dear David, it read, Deirdre phoned me last night to tell me what has happened. I am dreadfully sorry, especially as it is your last few days here. I do think that you should heed her warning. It pains me to write this but I have to agree with the advice that Deirdre tells me she has given to you. It is better that you make no attempt at contact while you are in Dargle. She will get in touch with you at your Dublin address as soon as she feels it is safe to do so. Come and see me before you go. Your good friend, Wilfred.

O chestnut tree, great-rooted blossomer,
Are you the leaf, the blossom or the bole
O body swayed to music, O brightening glance,
How can we know the dancer from the dance?
William Butler Yeats, Collected Poems

David, with clean shirt and collar had used a new blade for his morning shave, in spite of the risk of opening up old wounds. Shoes unusually shiny, he stepped out from his asylum home on his last round, and steering clear of the Superintendent's office, walked quickly until he reached the wards.

Everyone is polite now that I'm going ... and Deirdre has gone. Perhaps they are sorry. Not such a bad fellow they could be saying. Some of his sort are quite civilised. Take the Goldbergs. Good with figures too, I hear. Sister Eileen Fahy, handsome as ever, and proud of her Infirmary. So clean and modern, gives me a hug, a kiss and a cup of tea. Firm breasts are pressed against me, who has once been her child tucked up in her bed. Was anyone ever that happy the day Deirdre said yes? It's strange how leaving threatens some people while staying threatens others.

Throwing the Woodbine. He floated it in the air like a Frisbee discus and watched as it hovered over Vini's bed awaiting its fate. An acquired skill never to be used again. *Still, it might look good on the 'curriculum vitae.'*

David moved slowly through the ward saying goodbye to blood brothers: people he would never know except as symbols of a madness he was all too familiar with, Actors one grew fond of, not for who they are, but for the parts they play.

Never to be forgotten.

That Mahatma Ghandi gets on my nerves with his smugness and his public exhibitionism. I'll shove that tube up his other end;

see if he smiles then. Perhaps he would really like it that way round. Dirty bugger.

What's the incentive to leave for those lying on the mattresses? Perhaps they can't say good-bye because they have never said hello. Birth is so painful, especially if they can't conceive of any advantages for letting go, like sex or other treats. So what is the incentive for God's sake if you are nice and cosy in a sheltered world and ill informed about the other joys of life? How can you know that you are in a ghetto until you try to get out? Ask a priest, perhaps he will know the answer.

He passed the padded cells. All was quiet. Are you there, Cravich? David paused by the door.

When you protest that you want to get out they treat you as mad. When you stay in your padded world they say you are a strange creature. It could be your sixth sense is telling you what you don't want to know. Only an earthquake can change anything. Mine is telling me things as well (but for the grace of God there go I).

Sarah came out of her office to greet him.

"Your last round, Doctor. It feels like only a moment ago since your first round with the Superintendent."

"This ward does you credit. It looks like a palace. I'm going to miss my friends here."

... and you don't look half bad yourself now that you have recharged your batteries. Positively glowing again. And that smile, is that for me? It's better than a gold watch for a leaving present. You can see me looking at you. Hot as Anita Ekberg. What if I reached out now or better still, what if you were to reach out to me as you did then? Don't 'butter wouldn't melt in your mouth me.' I was there, naked, strung up and unafraid, stretching up to the peaks with all of you worshipping at my feet. I can smell the atmosphere as though we were in that room in the candlelight. First the priest and then me. It's like it all happened thousands of years ago ... yet I can feel myself being switched on at the click of a finger ... Just what happened to Fintan when he sniffed Deirdre's perfume.

"I'll give you one last piece of my mother's cake, David, if you sit down there and have a cup of tea with me before you are on your way." She pointed to the chair she had been sitting in and went to make the brew.

Now I am sure I know what happened to Fintan, This chair has her smell; it's vibrating from her body. I must get some air, and quickly before she comes back. He went over to the sink and douched his face in cold water.

"Here's your tea now, Doctor. I've told my mother how much you like her cake." She laughed. "But I won't tell you what she said." David drank the tea and wrapped the piece of cake in a napkin.

"Aren't mothers always right? I'll keep this for my journey when I can safely think about us." He moved close to her. Back against the wall, he pushed his body on to her, stamping her into his memory.

Which impression would he retain? They'd run the gamut from hot to cold. Her identity only expressed by the part she plays in other peoples dramas ... a nurse's lot, perhaps. Then he turned and left abruptly without another word.

His last call was to the Chief's office. He produced a brown paper bag from his briefcase and handed it over with a chuckle.

"You'll not have the last word on this, Doctor, for, I have the very same thing sat here in my drawer waiting for you to come and say goodbye." They both laughed heartily together as they exchanged presents.

"I can't say too much, Will, but you'll tell Deirdre I'll be waiting for her. That family of hers have underestimated her independence." David shook his head sadly. "My own heart is broken. That's all I will say just now."

Wilfred Behan reached out to comfort the young Doctor, then opened his brown paper bag and poured them both a glass. "I'll keep an eye on things, don't you worry. She is a rare jewel and can manage better than most, but we all need a bit of help now and again, so I'll do my best. It was time for her to step back into the big world out there, but she'll know that for herself without a doubt. A pity about her family, though." He shook his head sadly then downed the contents of his glass.

"They say that it's only the dead fish that swim with the tide, but prejudice does have a terrible power. Like the birds of Rhiannon it can cause people to forget its sting, for it comes in all disguises."

"You have a great understanding and courage, Wilfred. Did you know you have a namesake in the books I'm reading. A certain Wilfred Bion. At least Dr Reilly has the sense to hang on to you. But it's the next cattle boat to England they want me on. That's the beginning and end of it." David rose to go and the two men embraced again. They waved their brown paper bags to each other then David shut the door behind him.

On his way home he called in at the priest's house but got no reply to his knocking. When he arrived home Nellie was waiting for him. He saw that she had been crying. "I'm sorry to see you go, Doctor, and Miss Gillespie too. She is a fine woman and the talk we had gave me hope that I might be able to face the world again."

She handed him a small parcel neatly wrapped. "There's a little present of some blackberry jam for you both. I picked the berries myself." She wiped her eye briefly with a handkerchief which she had stuffed up her cardigan sleeve. "Try to think well of us here, for there's a mixture of good and bad in all of us."

"I'll always remember you, Nellie." David watched her walk along the pathway her bag clutched under her arm. She would share her story with her friend Finoola.

My arms are round you. I lean
against you, while the lark
Sings over us, and golden lights, and green
Shadows are on your bark,
There'll come a season when you'll stretch
Black boards to cover me:
Then in Mount Jerome I will lie, poor wretch,
With worms eternally.

With the first light of day David set off on his journey home. He stopped by the oak tree, took out his penknife and carved two letters in the wood where his car had removed the bark. Someone, a tourist meandering through the graveyard of a derelict asylum in twenty years or so, might cast a cold eye on the inscription. It would evoke nothing more than a flicker of curiosity. Outside the administration office he slowed down to a crawl. One brief glance back to the hospital buildings, already nothing more to him than stone chambers of memory, then away, out of the gates, down the steep hill and through the main street of Dargle. A lone taxi was stationed outside the Grand Hotel. The driver, unshaven, head slumped on his chest, waited hopefully in his half slumber for a fare. Abandoned sheets of last night's *Dargle Echo* scurried about the streets, footballs to the whimsy of the winds fancy, no longer the purveyors of fresh eagerly sought tidings. Yesterday's news. In two or maybe three minutes the town lay behind him.

He chose a circuitous route back to Dublin, not so much in a mood of hope that, by extending the journey, he might think of some excuse to turn back, but rather as a lingering caress on a journey of farewell. His affair with the Ireland he'd so much wanted to be part of was over. True, there was still so much to be said to the Chief and the Priest. Questions unanswered. But going back was not an option. He stopped at Cashel to rest for a while and feast his eyes on the majestic Cathedral, and wondered, if he were ever to return, whether his next visit would be as an ex pat. A tourist in his own country. Returnees were not welcome on a permanent basis. Two weeks' holiday in Kent made you a foreigner in Ireland.

His next stop was at a small cafe in Arklow. Over his cheese sandwiches he decided to head for Brittas Bay then look for a hotel to stop at.

There is only one bit of scenery that I'm really interested in, and she is in Dargle, so what's the point in all this tourist stuff, except that it's good training for my future life as a nomad? Or is all this a rehearsal for the final curtain, building up antibodies to the reapers final cut. Nothing to be done.

Along the white sands of Brittas he remembered his childhood swims. After the stony beach at Bray this was paradise. Always deserted; if money could not buy happiness it could certainly buy isolation. Undressed, he scanned the sand dunes then raced, eyes shut, into the cold sea. Between short spurts of breast stroke, underarm swimming, he stopped to look around and check for spies who might have hidden behind the sand dunes. As he dried himself with his socks he again considered the possibility of a return trip to Saint Elba's. Instead he drove through the Wicklow hills towards Glendalough and the small hamlet of Laragh. Across the tiny bridge near the small churchyard at the foot of Saint Kevin's Bed, he douched his face in the cool waters of the stream opposite to rid himself of journey's hangover. Above him the rocky ledge high up on the cliff had been a refuge from female company for the saint.

I should be so lucky as to find a foothold.

David smiled for the first time since leaving Dargle.

Being a saint is not my ambition either, thank God.

Through the Vale of Avoca where he found a small hotel set back from the road. Hotels like these reminded David of libraries. Thread quietly. A dream like atmosphere, the brain child of some escapist mind seeking asylum from the mainstream. He was an intruder, but without him they could not support their idyll. Once checked in he ordered a whiskey and went out into the hotel garden with it, returning shortly to replenish the glass.

"Another small one, Miss."

She is the same woman that showed me to my room. Now she serves the drinks. Maybe she is also the cook or even the chamber maid. Try not to look, but it's that official uniform with its white formal blouse and the green cotton skirt that makes her appear so seductively unavailable. Yes, she is the receptionist as well.

His second drink downed in a gulp, David ordered a third. As he handed the money to her he gave the young woman a smile, amused, as she mocked him back with her eyes. *The power that women have over men.* After an early dinner he climbed the stairs to his room.

Restless, he tossed and turned between day dream and half sleep. He was back again in the asylum grounds behind the high wall in search of the priest's house. Finding it hard to locate he realised that it had become detached from the Church building and now stood in its own grounds. A flag hung from the second floor window. Its cream and black colours flapped noisily in the wind. Through the window he caught a glimpse of Deirdre. She stood with her back to him. In his attempt to get closer he was impeded by a snake like arm as Vini emerged from the shadows, his limb waving its way rapaciously backwards and forwards in front of David's face; in search of booty, like a bird of prey. It grew longer and longer as he watched, mesmerised by its actions. He lunged forward beneath the limb and managed to get closer to the window. As he did so he saw Deirdre's face reflected in the mirror inside the priest's sitting room. In front of her facing the window stood Fintan. His tall body, dressed in a black cassock, towered over her like a gigantic hawk. Deirdre remained still as the priest pulled her black sweater over her head. Suddenly the cleric was kneeling down in front of her as though in worship and David could see in the mirror two large hands grasping her breasts above the bowed head as the double jointed priest tried to hide from his own actions. Deirdre bent backwards, her whole body erupting in a paroxysm of excitement. The path to her door was blocked, this time by the figure of the Mahatma Ghandi who pushed the rubber tube feeder at him, insistently pointing to his open mouth. As he grasped at the tube it began to move in his hands, wriggling about until it gradually assumed a life of its own. Each time he tried to move closer to the door the venomous head threatened him. Desperate to confront Deirdre and the priest he drove himself forward, both arms braced over his face to prevent himself being strangled. Now he could see the crouching figure of the cleric imprison the young woman in his grip as he directed her breasts towards his gaping lips. Deirdre reached forward to guide her nipple and massage its milk into the gasping mouth beneath her. Suddenly from the darkness "Shmegegge, shmendrick, shmuck." David heard Cravich's voice rant its torrent of abuse as the ominous figure of the Jew blocked his progress. He looked for the padded cell door to slam it shut and called out to Wilfred to come to his rescue.

He awoke abruptly out of the dream and turned on the light. The sound of the river outside calmed him. The hotel was still, and for a moment David thought he might go in search of comfort from the woman who had attracted him earlier that evening. Instead he heated the kettle and made himself a cup of tea in the small pot that had been neatly laid out with some biscuits on a bedside tray.

I've not just lost my dream, I"ve gained a nightmare. Is this what happens when roots are weakened? Suppose I return to Saint Elba's and find it has already passed into history? No doubt some kind person would find a cosy padded cell for me somewhere else. Am I the mad one to look for acceptance in their country? But why should I be driven to England or beyond when I've only just arrived in this green land? Delusions of Irishness! Delusions of Asylum. Perhaps there really is a cure, and Deirdre and myself can stay together. Maybe spend a holiday in the Dordogne sampling the flavours of roasted red peppers and youthful red wine. On return we can buy a little house in the country and a tasteful terrace in Dargle overlooking the river and hang the rats. No doubt Deirdre would be discovered and join the Gate theatre with Michael MacLiammoir and Hilton Edwards. Then Juno and the Paycock at the Abbey. What happens if fortune plays you a good hand and it's not just a trick? It's not good for people to live in each other's pockets so we would not be too near the Gillespies. Of course there might be nachas frum kinder to help win over them over. They'll be attracted by seeing their own image reproduced yet again. The Commonwealth of Gillespies. But what if they have Semitic features? What then? God forbid, that this should happen to the Gillespies. Such a nice family. He ran his hand over his nose and scowled. I can see why the outcasts have resorted to bombs.

David slept till he heard a woman's voice call out for breakfast to be taken.

Is she the boot boy as well for heavens sake?

His mouth was still full of the flavours of his dreams of Dordogne but as he dressed his mood of depression returned.

In France, too, they had 'watered their tree of freedom with the blood of the Jews'.

No nearer to an answer to his problems he went down for breakfast.

Would there would be a message from Deirdre waiting for him when he got home?

Fintan shook hands with Deirdre, holding on to her as he lowered himself down into the chair opposite her at a small corner table in Corrigans Limited. The table where David used to wait for her. His crew's nest. Now she could see things through his eyes. For better or worse, their vision united. There was no going back. The priest beamed at her.

"I'm glad you could meet me again outside Saint Elba's. That night at Mulligan's was as bad as the worst of the things that have befallen me in my life."

"All that is behind us now." She removed her hand from his and patted him on the arm. She wasn't sure where his mind had settled. "Sit over here, beside me. It's a bit like old times, getting together again like this, except for one thing of course."

Early evening trade was in full swing. The pianist's repertoire had reached out beyond the memory span of its more youthful clientele as he thumped out his individual rendition of 'You're the cream in my coffee'.

"The sights here would test the resolve of a saint, never mind a humble parish priest, like myself. Whoever wrote the Bible or set out the rules of abstinence for us poor mortals could not have seen these samples of the beauty of God's work." The priest sighed.

"I can see you're heading down the path of laicization my friend, or do I misjudge your words?" Deirdre sipped her whiskey, shaking her head to decline Fintan's offer to replenish her glass.

"You might think this a little odd, my dear," he glowed once again, "but now I feel I have a choice of my own in the matter, the issue seems to have changed." The priest leaned back, putting his arms together behind his head, giving a glimpse of the grey shirt and clerical collar under the unbuttoned double breasted jacket. "When I decide, it won't be out of blind ignorance or even a blind faith. Vocation is a misused idea and this time I'll consider what the job could mean and what I'm wanting and able to give it. You see, I've eaten the forbidden fruit and I'm the better man for it! Does that surprise you?" He leaned over towards her, lapels truly parted, his spiritual identity now clearly exposed under his jacket. "But here I am going on about myself. How are you coping away from the old asylum and your David?"

"That's the trouble, Fintan." She noticed he'd developed a tidy looking pot-belly under his habit. "I'm not too sure he is my David, though he'll always be that in here." She put her hand under her sweater and rotated it in a massaging movement. "It's right in my heart that I feel the pain, and other places too."

"Have you been in touch?" Fintan's asked, sitting back in his seat. His self-satisfied expression had vanished with the question.

"I don't think we should make David the subject of this little reunion." Deirdre saw the priest flinch. "It's not that I don't trust you, Fintan, but I am a bit unsure about where you stand. Someone has been talking to my family and they have not let me out of their sight since I left the hospital."

"Oh, surely that's a bit far-fetched?" The priest was frowning.

"I seem to remember that is your standard response when there is something going on that you don't feel able to able to deal with."

"You haven't forgiven me, that's the answer." He shook his head sadly. "Look what happens when I do try to come out, I behave like a monk on a day's outing. No, my dear, I'm not so much a coward as an ignoramus with insight."

Deirdre looked at Fintan. "It's time you started to learn the facts of life for yourself. Chicago is not the only place that the Mafia hang out." Her eyes drawn again to his belly bulge. It may have been there before but it had not been so assertively protuberant. Of that she was sure. "I've a feeling you are an addict to your innocence." She stood up abruptly, the priest no longer the centre of her attention. "Let's get out of here and quick."

Fintan gulped down his drink. "What's the matter? Is it something I've said?" He looked out of the pub window to where Deirdre was pointing. "Or is one of the family heading this way?"

Grabbing the priest by the arm she hauled him to his feet. "That is exactly what I'm trying to avoid." She pointed again at a shining red Jaguar that had drawn up outside the bar. "It's Peader Murphy and his pals. Aren't my parents wanting me to make him one of the family, for God's sake. Come on, we're out of the side door. He is not the cream in my coffee, and never will be."

On their way out Deirdre noticed that the poster of Bogart had been removed to make room for The Stones.

"Has no one said those daring
Kind eyes should be more learn'd?
Or warned you how despairing
The moths are when they are burned?
I could have warned you; but you are young,
So we speak a different tongue."

Father and son headed towards Dublin airport. The misty October morning matched the scum gray color of the River Liffey as its heavy shadows heralded winter over the city. Neither spoke as they drove past landmarks that had once been so familiar they had gone unnoticed. Would those memories last, preserved in the rarified atmosphere of his exiles nostalgia, vintage 69? Mummified like those ancient corpses of Michan's Church. Preserved in the smell of Bewley's coffee and the tincture of formaldehyde from Baggot Street Hospital's morgue. Now they looked away to avoid the pain of memory attached to them.

"Perhaps, son, we were intended to keep wandering. That's why we haven't found the promised land till now. The people that are settling there will be a different race to the rest of us. Will even they want us as we are?"

Bernard Benn had taken out his rusty rifle from the bottom of the bedroom wardrobe and fired a few imaginary shots when the tanks had rolled into the Gaza strip. Then he'd seen himself reflected in the mirror. "It's being temporary residents that has kept us on our toes."

He put his arm around David's shoulder then reluctantly removed it as the traffic thickened. He drove north, past the Gresham Hotel where light-hearted visitors rejoiced in the traveller's freedom of voluntary mobility. Guide books flashing, they could look forward to seeing the sights, then return home to bore their loved ones with photographs of Guinness's Brewery.

"England is only across the water, as they say, so I'll be seeing you often. Soon you'll be able to come back home, I'm sure. Aren't you as Irish as I am, and I've spent my whole life here? Even your grandfather, olivasholim, lived half his life in the auld sod. You've got as much right to live here as the next person, though I suppose not all of them here accept that, do they?"

He pointed to the Rotunda Hospital as they crawled through the heavy morning traffic. "How many babies did you deliver when you were a student there?" He waved proudly towards maternity hospital where his son had been a student.

It's a no hands on the steering wheel morning. Still we seem set fair. Due north north west at a guess.

Reluctantly, David looked up from his side seat navigation, trying to shake off his own morning sickness. "We were more like the babies ourselves, as far as I remember. Sitting around the bedside in the tenement houses playing poker while the midwife did all the work. Then a speedy return, forceps waving, to the hospital to get the credit and down a few pints over tales of breech deliveries the like of which had never before been witnessed." He glanced across to see how his father was coping, wondering what he would do if he told him to turn back. There was still time to change his mind, after all.

"You'll miss your friends from Dargle, and especially Deirdre, I suppose. Will you be writing to her, I wonder, son?" Getting no reply he went on. "Maybe things will change before long. In my day we all lived in a ghetto with no mixing at all." His own brother had married out, an uncle that David had never met. "Now it's not that uncommon, even over the border in Ulster, for one religion to transfuse itself with the blood of another." He patted his son's arm. Being a Jew was a bit like having TB. "I've no doubt that your young lady will be off to England soon. Ask her to drop in on me before she goes." Mr.

Benn rambled on, creating his own vision of the grandchildren he might never see.

They drove through Drumcondra. The north side of Dublin a foreign place to those who dwelt on the opposite bank of the Liffey. Soon the city was behind them. Slowing his speed as he reached the airport, where so many mothers and fathers had bid good-bye to their offspring, perhaps never to see them again, he looked around at his only son.

"I'll be back, don't you worry!" David avoided his father's gaze. They parked the car and crossed the busy road to the terminal building.

"I remember when this place was not much bigger than that tiny airport near the hospital you worked at. Just a few planes a day. Now you can fly to the far corners of the earth from here. Not many hiding places left."

David checked in his suitcases.

Those uniforms again. At least they can be sure of work with their fathers in the right places, not that it's very glamorous having to smile at sweaty men smelling of deodorant ten thousand feet up. Don't think you've got rid of me so easy.

The young doctor turned to say good bye to his closest living relative.

"It's not an airport at all but a bloody crematorium. A cruel transfiguration assisted by women in green uniforms supplied by Aer Linctus. Put a few tourists on the plane with a free sandwich and no one will know that it is a cattle truck exporting its human cargo out of sight."

Syphilis, suicide and schizophrenia. So Long. Don't be bitter.

"Any good tips now, and I'll expect you to phone me; before the race and not after, mind you. I'll have my head stuck in books again. Freud and Melanie Klein, and not the racing form guide." He kept his voice steady. "Keep your eyes off the women, da." David called out as the sprightly figure of his father walked through the doors, swinging his arms from both shoulders in his familiar way. This time his son noticed the stoop in his father's back.

David watched the coastline fade into the distance. He sat, wondering if the seagulls, that screeched unheard below the belly of the plane, would stay with them for the whole journey or hand over to their English equivalent half way. Already he struggled to recapture his passion for the country that had vanished from view. His mother, long gone, and his lost sister. Those wounds had scabbed over but his father ... too much what he himself was for the wound ever to heal.

The block was chipped and could never be repaired. For his Jewish brothers who stayed behind, content in their Ghetto. Good luck. Don't make the mistake of trying to be one of them. They don't mind you until you try to cross the border. He was clear now that the priest had approached him as he would a doctor he wanted to consult with. He had the understanding of the needs of an outsider and the power that his welcome exerted over a stranger. Deirdre was the border that he'd crossed. When they saw he wanted integration the worm turned, like the Catholics in the North, acceptable in the ghetto. If only they hadn't made trouble by looking for equal rights.

Through the clear skies he saw the Bristol Channel in the distance. David signalled the hostess and ordered two whiskies. "Glenmorangie, if you've got it. One for the young lady sitting over there and one for myself." He shook his head. "On the rocks if we may."

Deirdre raised her glass across the corridor, whispering to herself. "We've crossed over at last. God be with us who ever you are." She sipped her Scotch, tentatively at first. "Different, without a doubt." She lowered the remains in one gulp.

End Here.

Mememorme.

Lightning Source UK Ltd.
Milton Keynes UK
UKOW041324160513

210790UK00001B/6/P